OTHER EVER AFTERS

This book was drawn with Polychromos colored pencils on Bristol board and hand-lettered with Microns.

Copyright © 2022 by Melanie Gillman

All rights reserved. Published in the United States by RH Graphic, an imprint of Random House Children's Books, a division of Penguin Random House LLC, New York.

RH Graphic with the book design is a trademark of Penguin Random House LLC.

Visit us on the web! RHKidsGraphic.com • @RHKidsGraphic

Educators and librarians, for a variety of teaching tools, visit us at RHTeachersLibrarians.com

Library of Congress Cataloging-in-Publication Data is available upon request.
ISBN 978-0-593-30319-1 (hardcover) — ISBN 978-0-593-30318-4 (pbk.)
ISBN 978-0-593-30321-4 (ebook)

Designed by Patrick Crotty

MANUFACTURED IN CHINA
10 9 8 7 6 5 4 3 2 1
First Edition

A comic on every bookshelf.

OTHER EVER AFTERS

NEW QUEER FAIRY TALES
BY MELANIE GILLMAN

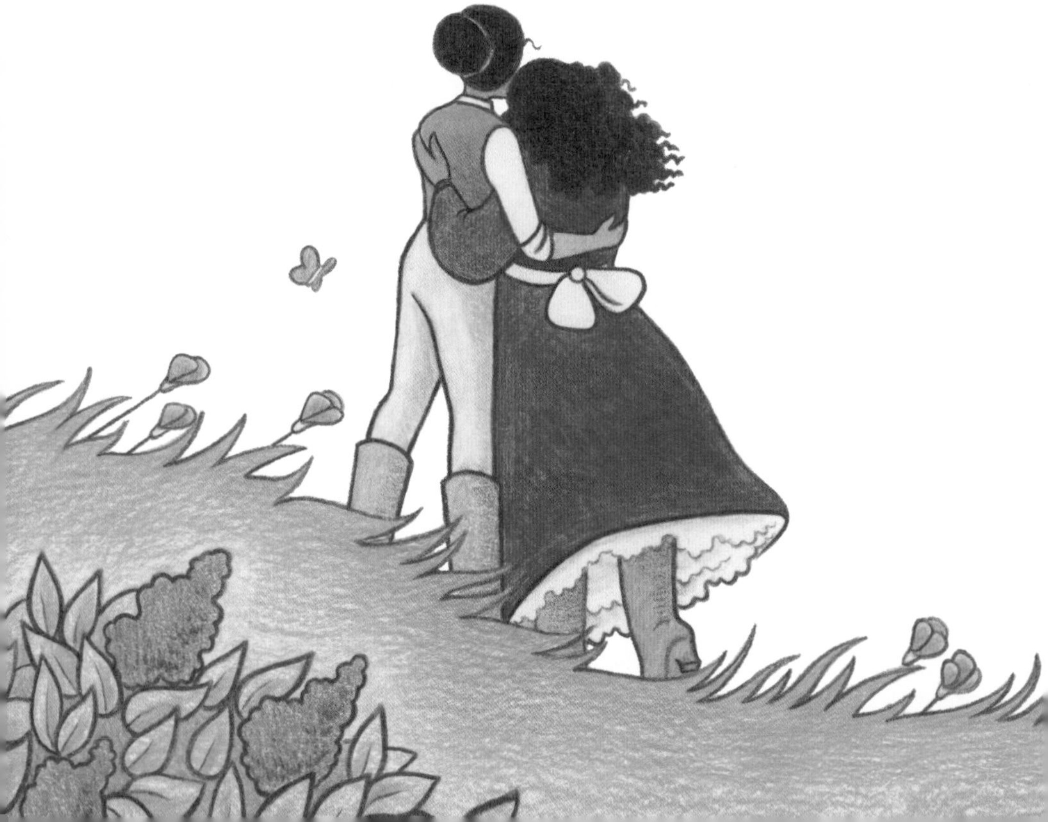

CONTENTS

INTRODUCTION

We all know (for we are told it so often) that girls must make journeys.

Leaving their families,

and entering the deep, dark,

dangerous woods.

Evading beasts,
staying to the path,
and spurning temptations.

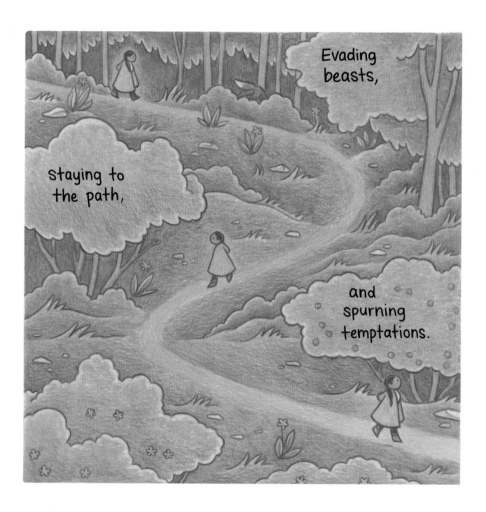

At the end of
the woods is a
clearing.

And in that
clearing, a
grand castle,

where she
will marry

and rule.

These stories are told
for a reason.

THE KING'S FOREST

I am a ranger in the King's forest.

It's a very important job.

A magic flower grows only in the forest—and could easily be taken by a—

POACHER!!!

PUT THAT BACK.!!
This?

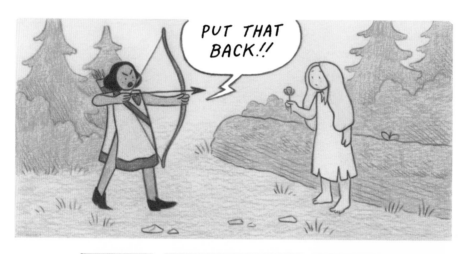

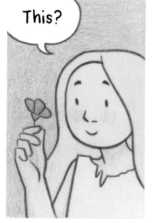

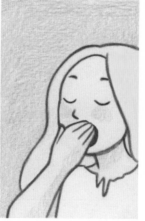

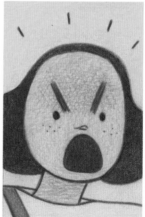

You're in trouble!!
The King says people'll gobble up all the magic flowers!
Then there won't be any left!!
King's wrong.
Magic flowers like knowing when people need them.
If you pick one but leave the root, two more will grow in its place.

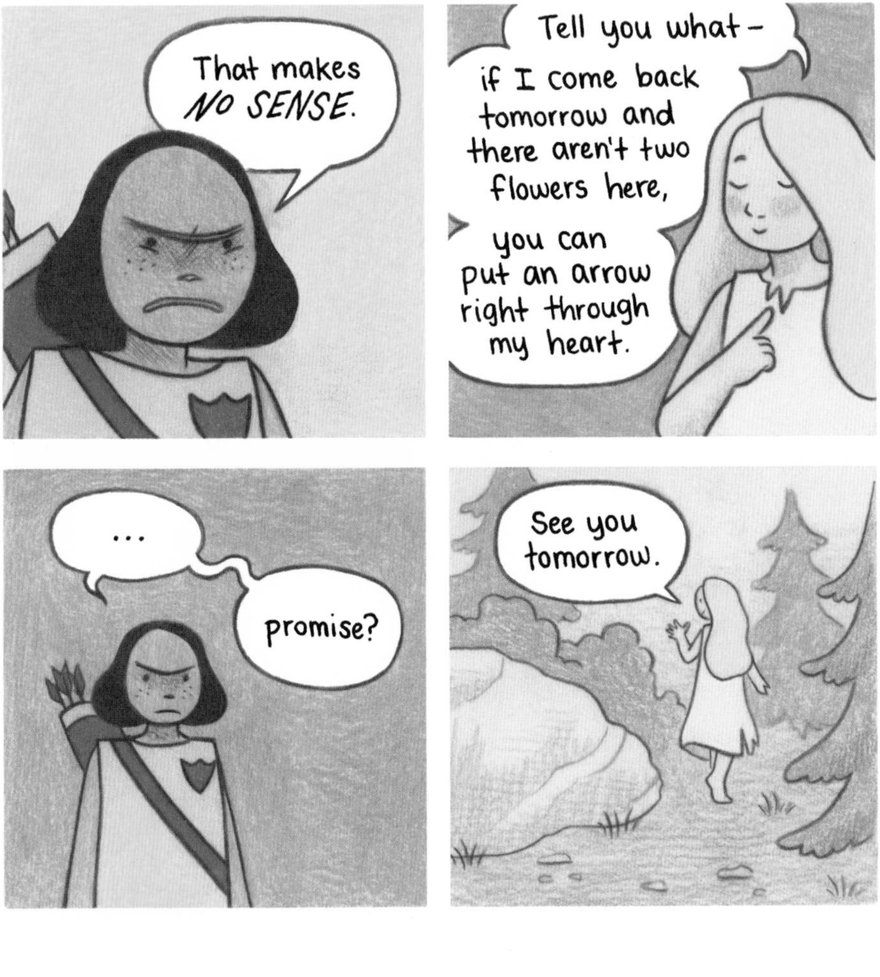
That makes NO SENSE.
Tell you what–
if I come back tomorrow and there aren't two flowers here,
you can put an arrow right through my heart.
...
promise?
See you tomorrow.

I realized too late I'd invited her to trespass again tomorrow.
I'm the WORST RANGER.

You're still breaking the law.

I'm not scared of the law.

You know what is scary?

The BEAST of the FOREST.

It's got a coat the color of blood,

and claws as black as tar,

and ten sulfur horns on its head,

and it hunts Children for fun.

That's stupid. I know everything about the forest.

I'd know if there was a beast.

But clearly you *don't* know everything about the forest.

See you tomorrow!

The King's forest has birds, foxes, and deer.

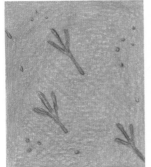 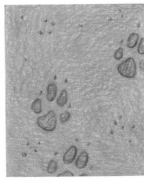 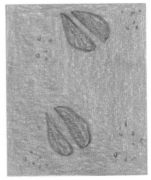

(Which sometimes come *very* close to your tent at night.)

~crnch~

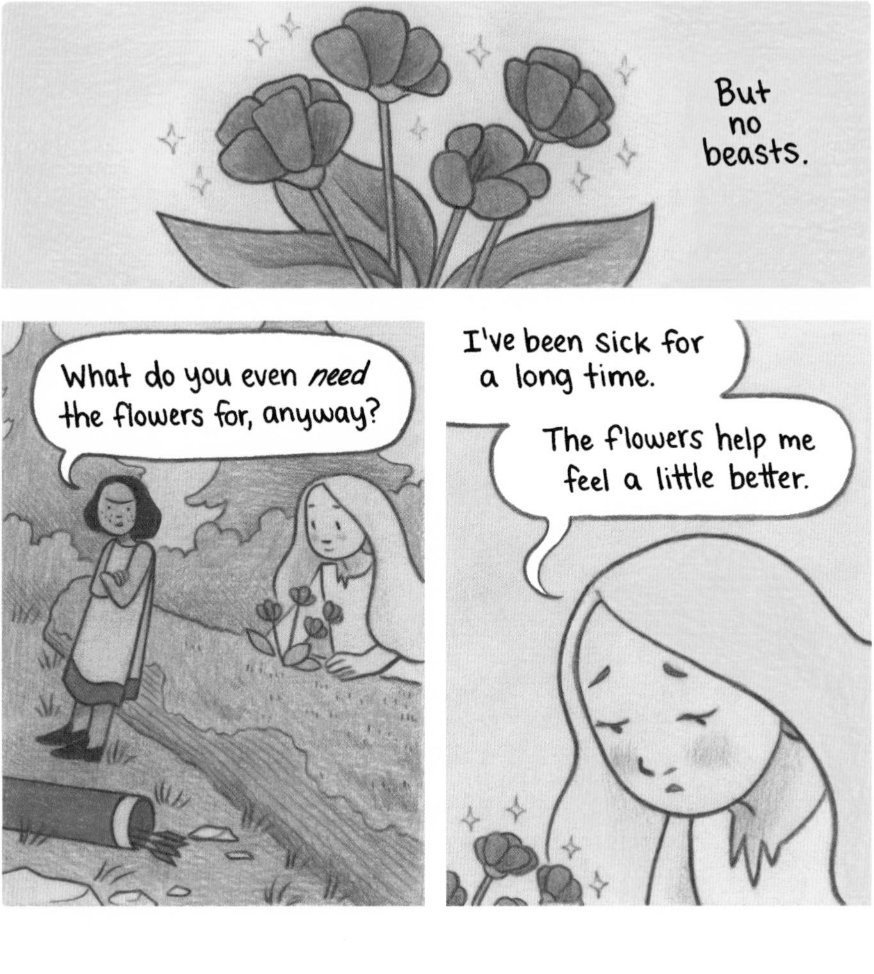
But no beasts.
What do you even *need* the flowers for, anyway?
I've been sick for a long time.
The flowers help me feel a little better.

Do you think the King is sick, too?

What?

Is that why he doesn't let anyone else take the flowers?

I don't think so. I've never actually seen him in here.

Oh.

Do you think it makes you pretty, too?
What?
NOTHING

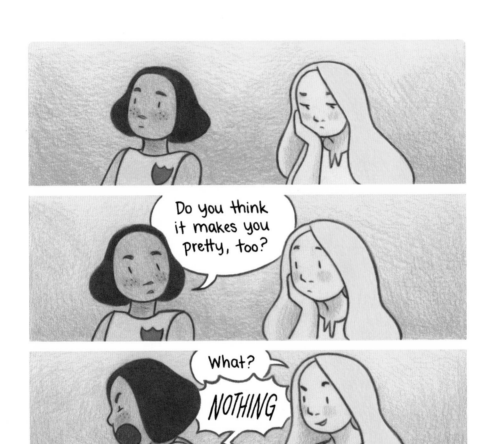

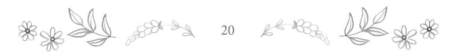

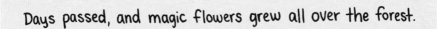

Days passed, and magic flowers grew all over the forest.

On patrols, I looked for claw marks in the soil.

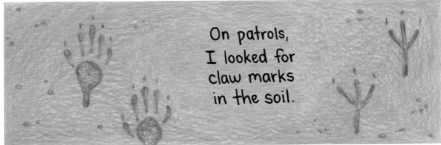

But saw no signs of a beast.

I don't think there *is* a beast.
There is.
I would've found its tracks if it was real.
It's tricky. It can disguise itself as other animals.

What does it even *want?*
I think... it's greedy.
It likes when people are sick.
It'll be angry when it finds out I've been taking so many flowers.

Why don't you just leave, then? Take your flowers and run!

Some things are worth a little risk.

The next day, I found a new set of tracks.

Horses—
many
horses.

Not a
beast at
all!

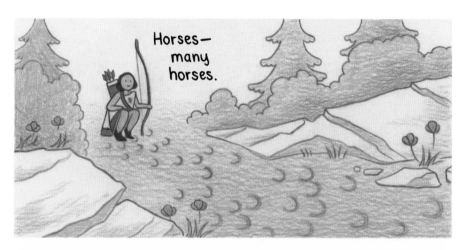

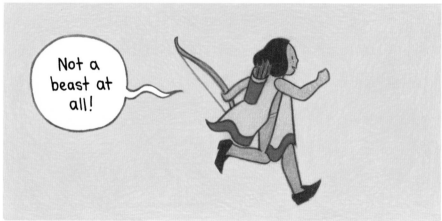

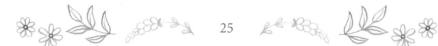

It's just the-

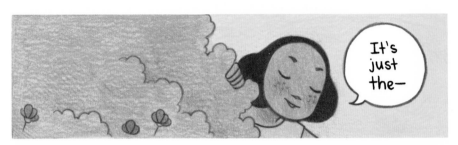

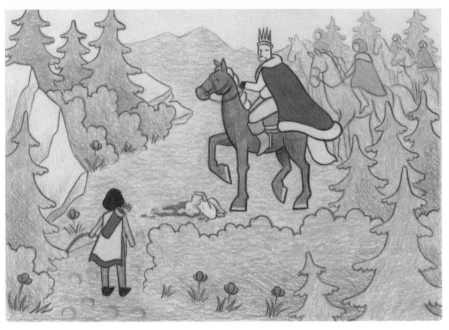

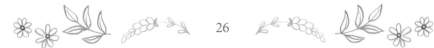

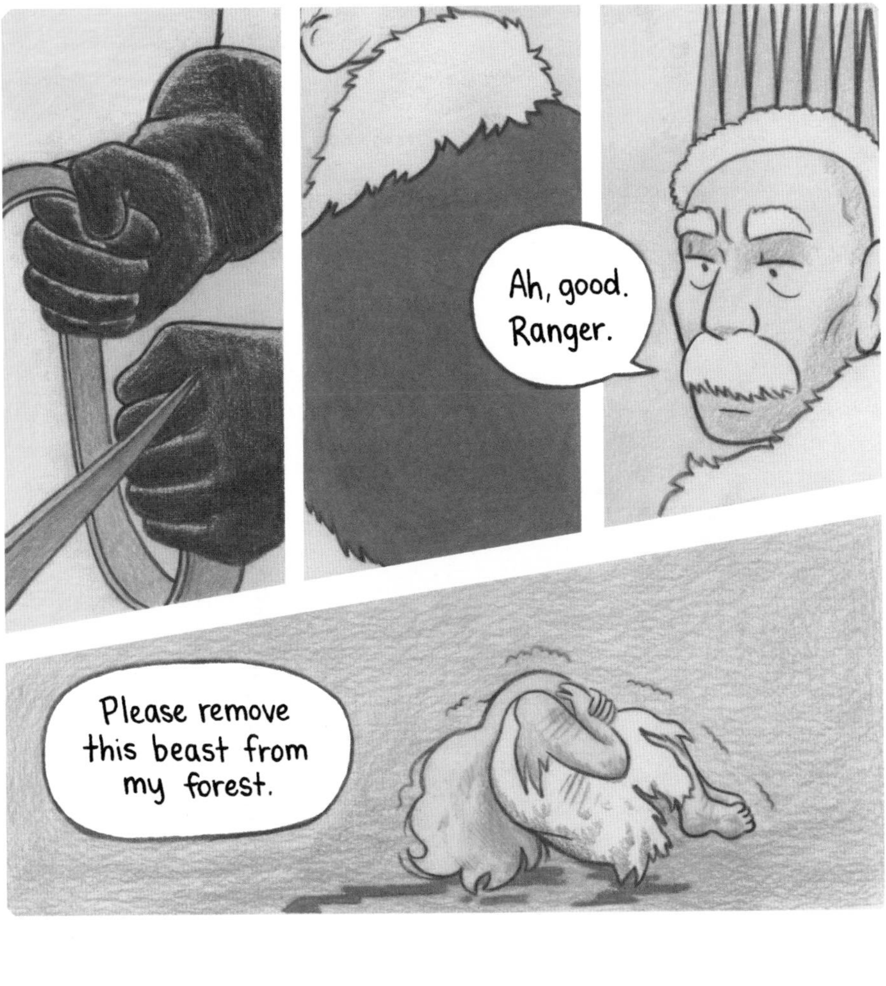
Ah, good. Ranger.
Please remove this beast from my forest.

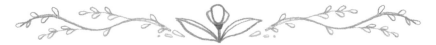

I will.

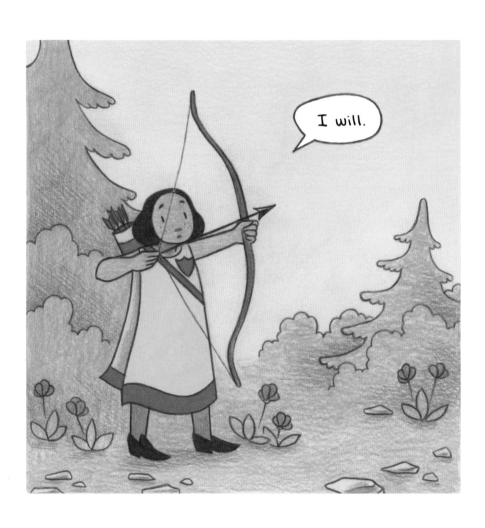

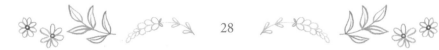

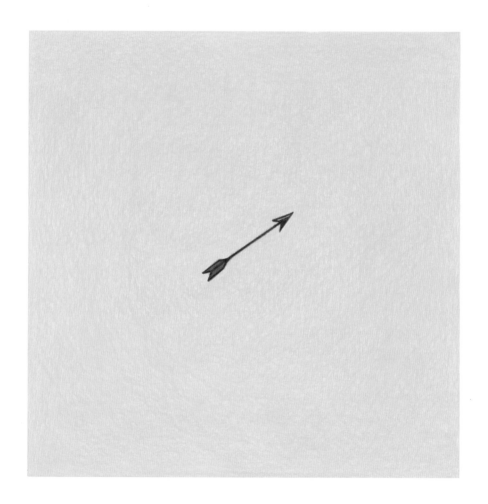

THE GOOSE GIRL

I am the princess of a vast kingdom.

Sixth of my name on my mother's side.

I have riches, land, servants, title.

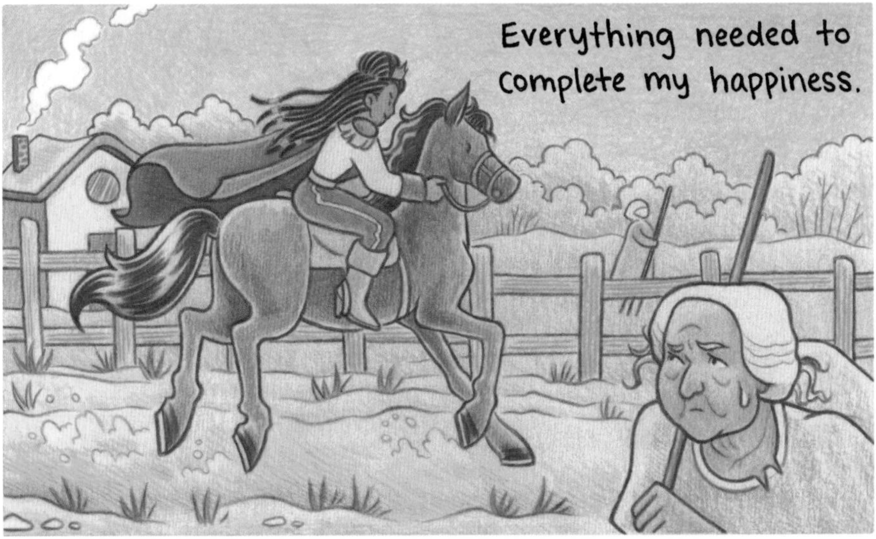
Everything needed to complete my happiness.

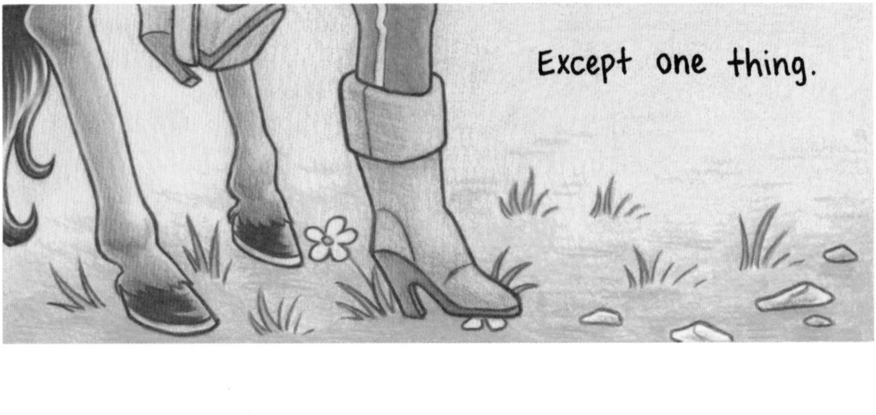
Except one thing.

Goose Girl.

Though your station is low and your family poor,

I have watched you selling your geese at the market,

and your beauty has bewitched me.

Be my bride, and I will share with you all that I possess.

My castle, my wealth, my hunts, my feasts.

Only complete my happiness, and I swear, I will complete yours.

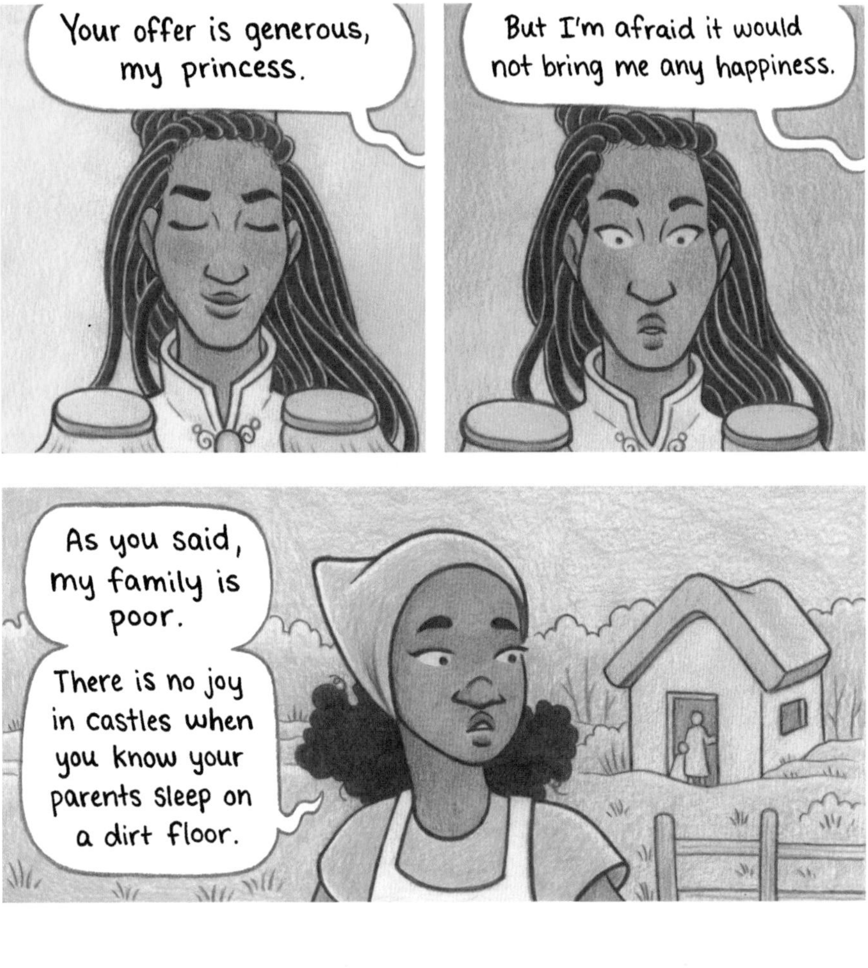
Your offer is generous, my princess.
But I'm afraid it would not bring me any happiness.
As you said, my family is poor.
There is no joy in castles when you know your parents sleep on a dirt floor.

Nor succor in feasts when your siblings go hungry.

And I'm afraid, no love in a wife who would ask her beloved to live in such a way.

This is...

MADNESS??

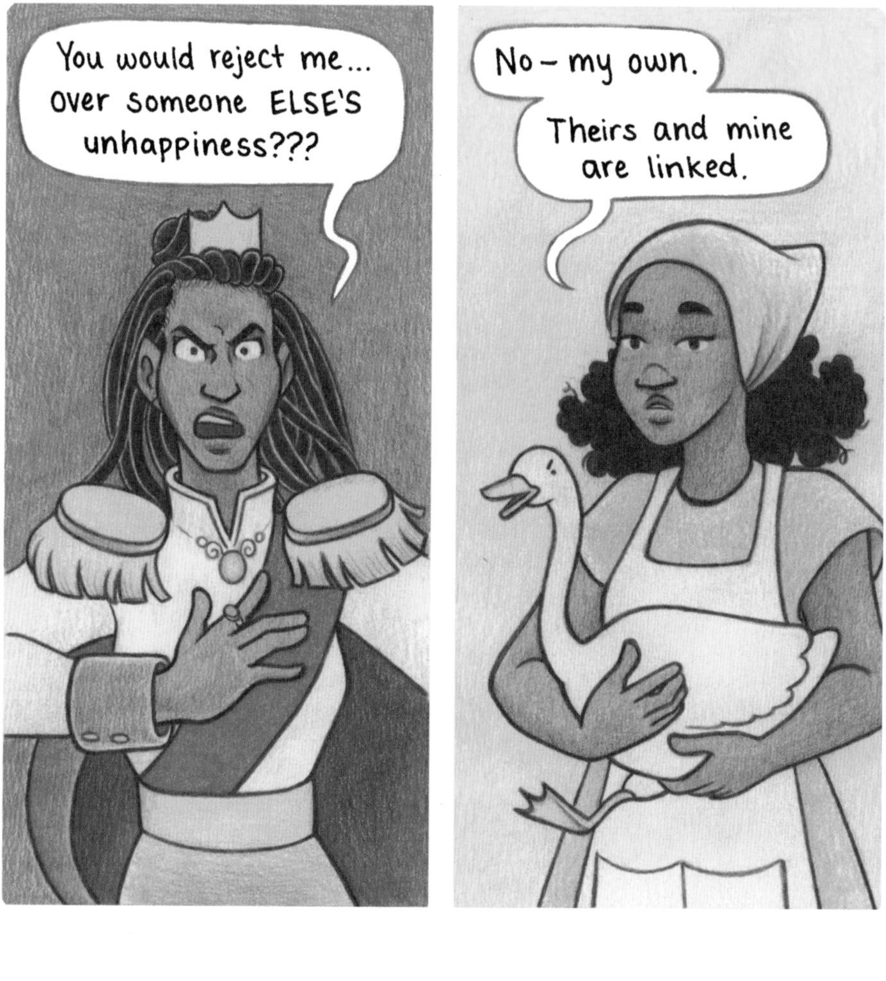
You would reject me...
over someone ELSE'S
unhappiness???
No - my own.
Theirs and mine
are linked.

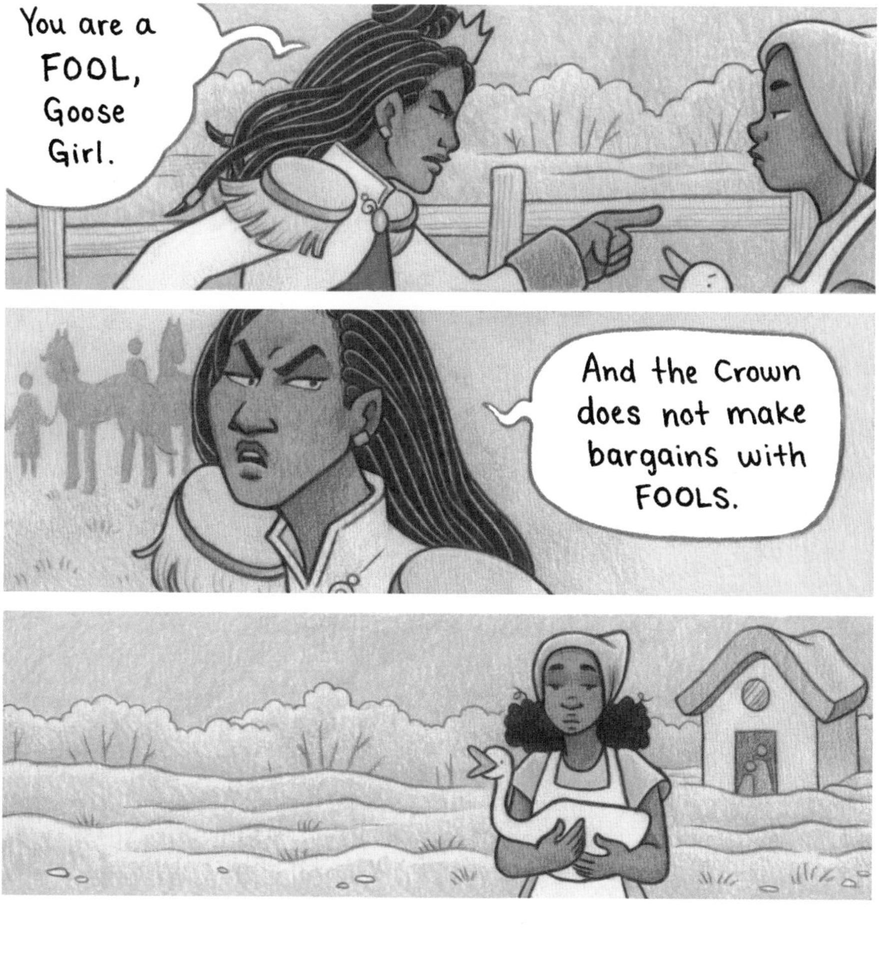
You are a FOOL, Goose Girl.
And the Crown does not make bargains with FOOLS.

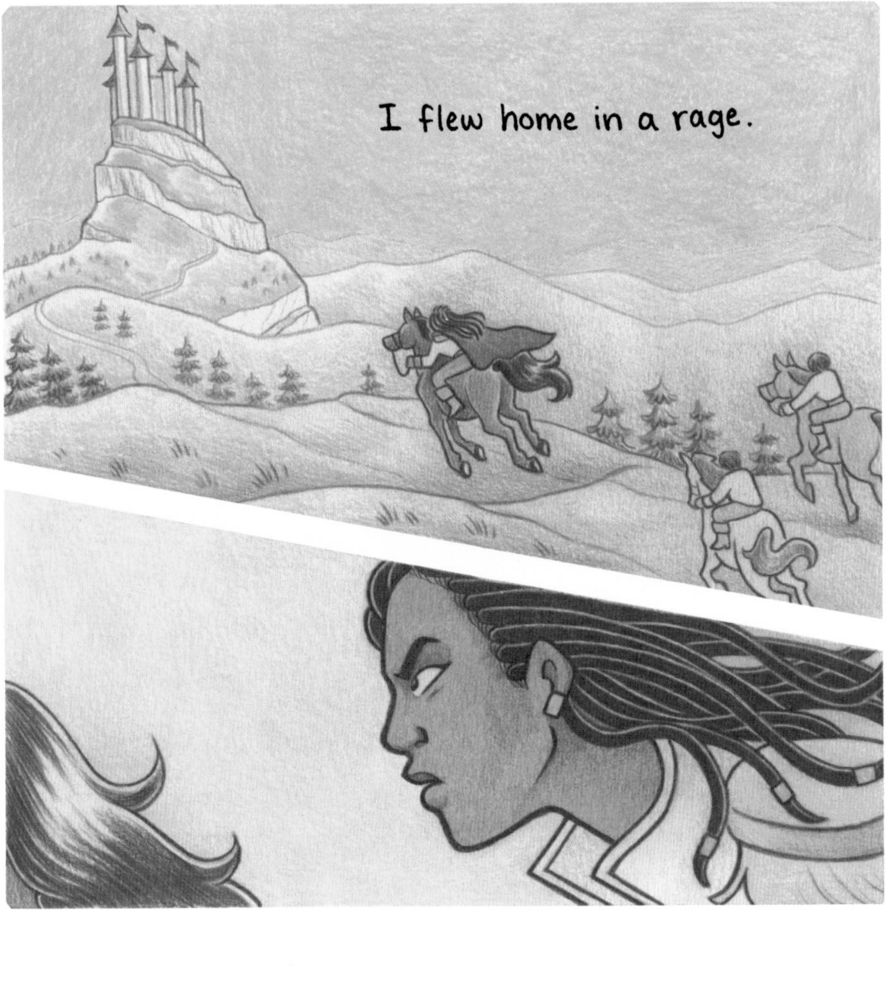
I flew home in a rage.

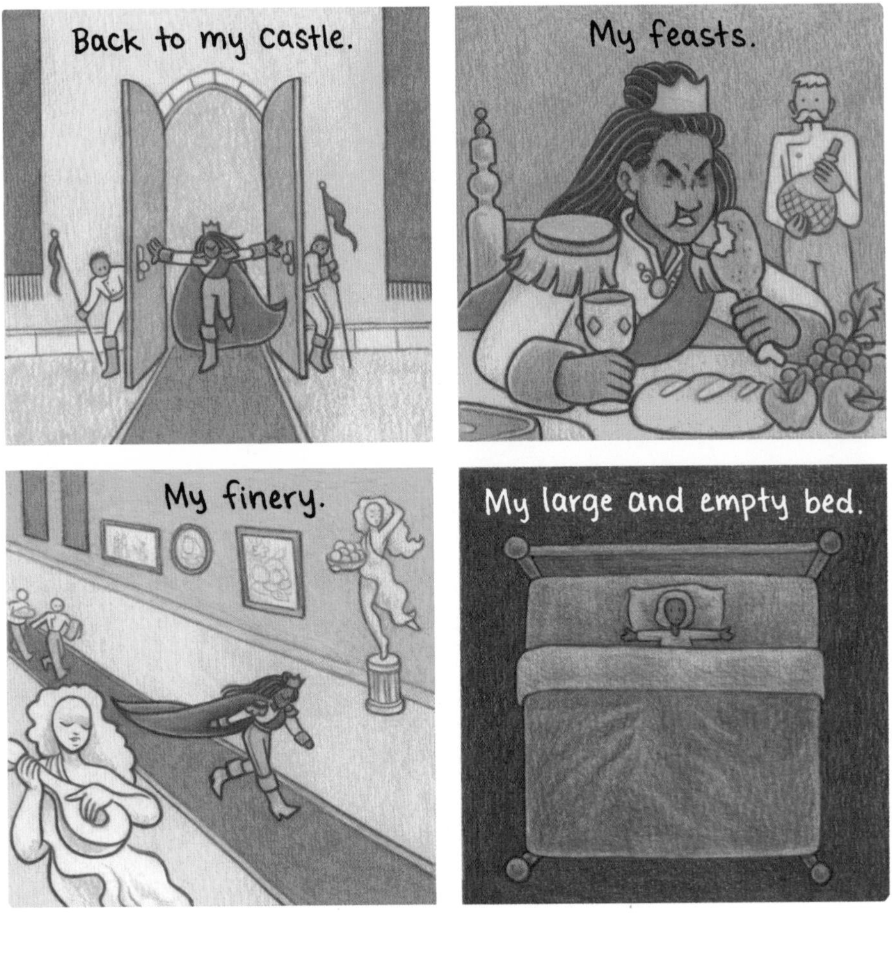
Back to my castle.
My feasts.
My finery.
My large and empty bed.

Madness...

To think that I... the most powerful woman in the kingdom...

...would tolerate living with only incomplete happiness!

GOOSE GIRL!!!

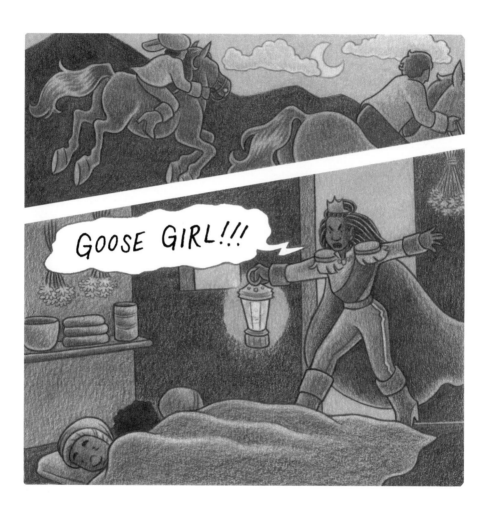

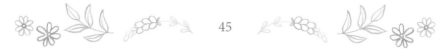

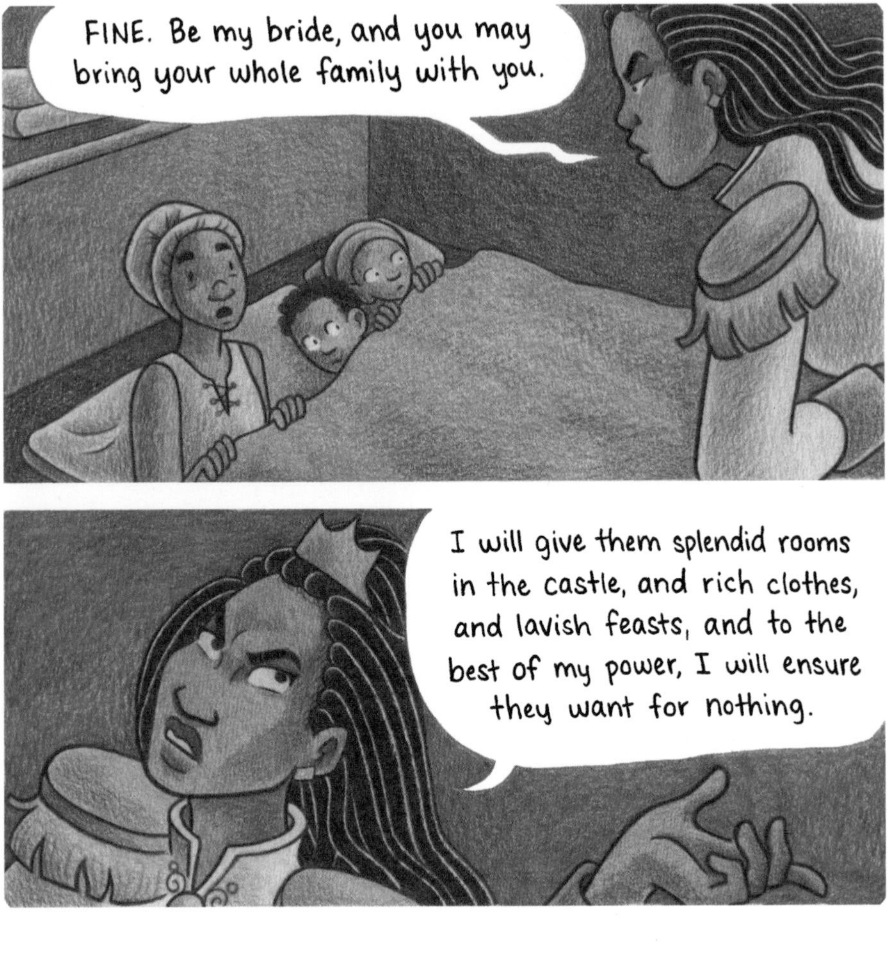
FINE. Be my bride, and you may bring your whole family with you.
I will give them splendid rooms in the castle, and rich clothes, and lavish feasts, and to the best of my power, I will ensure they want for nothing.

Your offer is generous, but—

But?!

—but I'm afraid it would not complete our happiness.

There is no joy in feasts when the food was grown by people who starve.

Nor warmth in splendid rooms when just outside a nation sleeps in the cold.

For all your wealth, the only dowry you've offered me—

—is an empty chest.

You ...

DARE ...

CALL MY GENEROSITY EMPTY ???

You would turn me down-
condemn your whole family to poverty-
for PRIDE??

It is not I who condemns my family to poverty, Princess.

What is this
feeling?

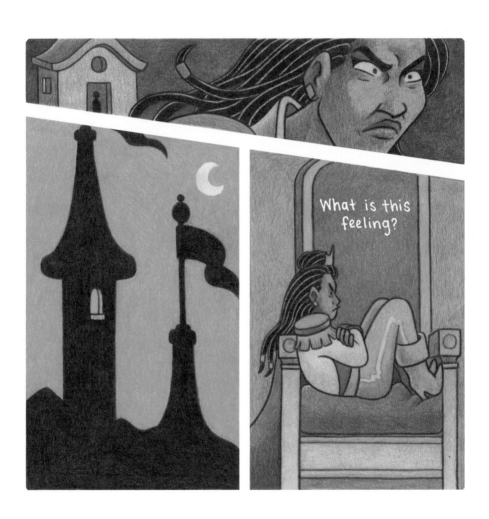

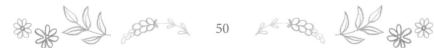

I have everything else I could possibly want.

Surely, *surely*, that's enough?

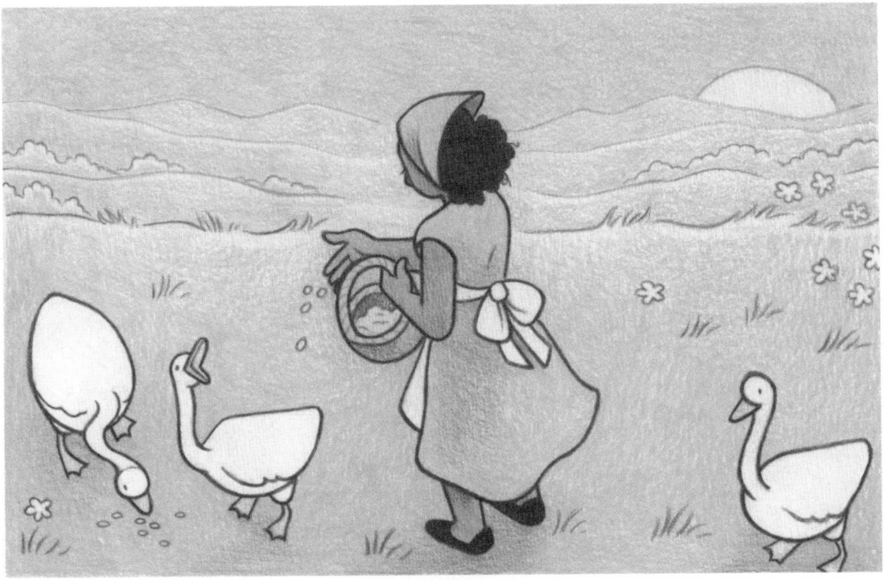

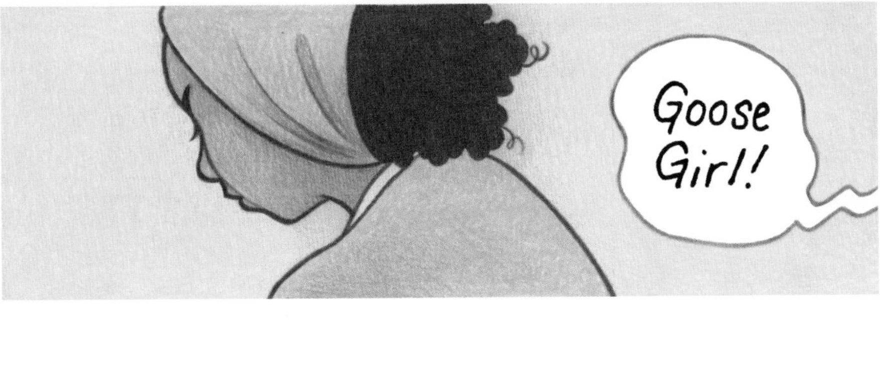
Goose Girl!

FINE.
Here is my offer.
Marry me, and I will open up the treasury to the whole kingdom.
I'll build roads and schools and libraries and hospitals in every village.

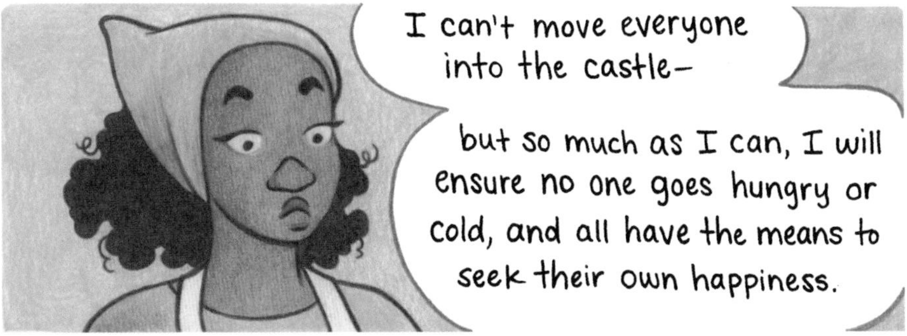
I can't move everyone into the castle-
but so much as I can, I will ensure no one goes hungry or cold, and all have the means to seek their own happiness.

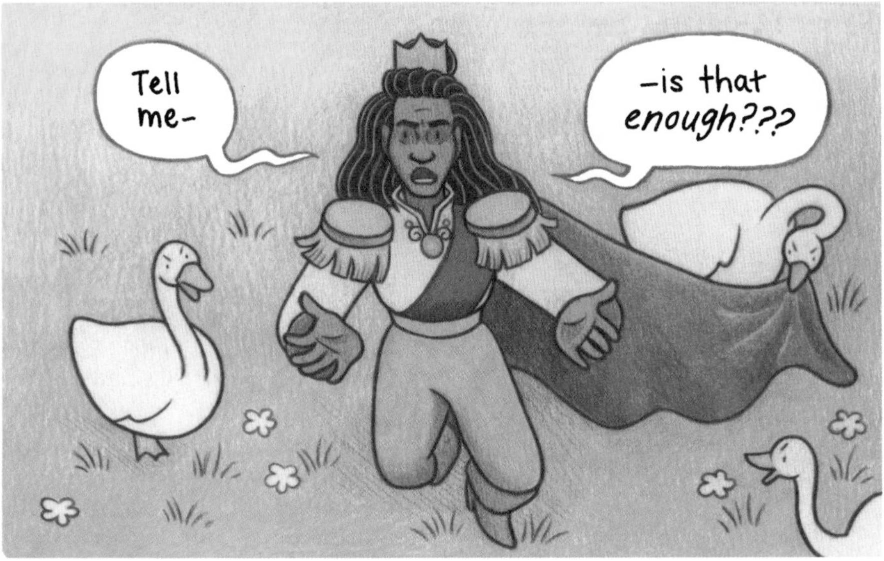
Tell me-
-is that *enough???*

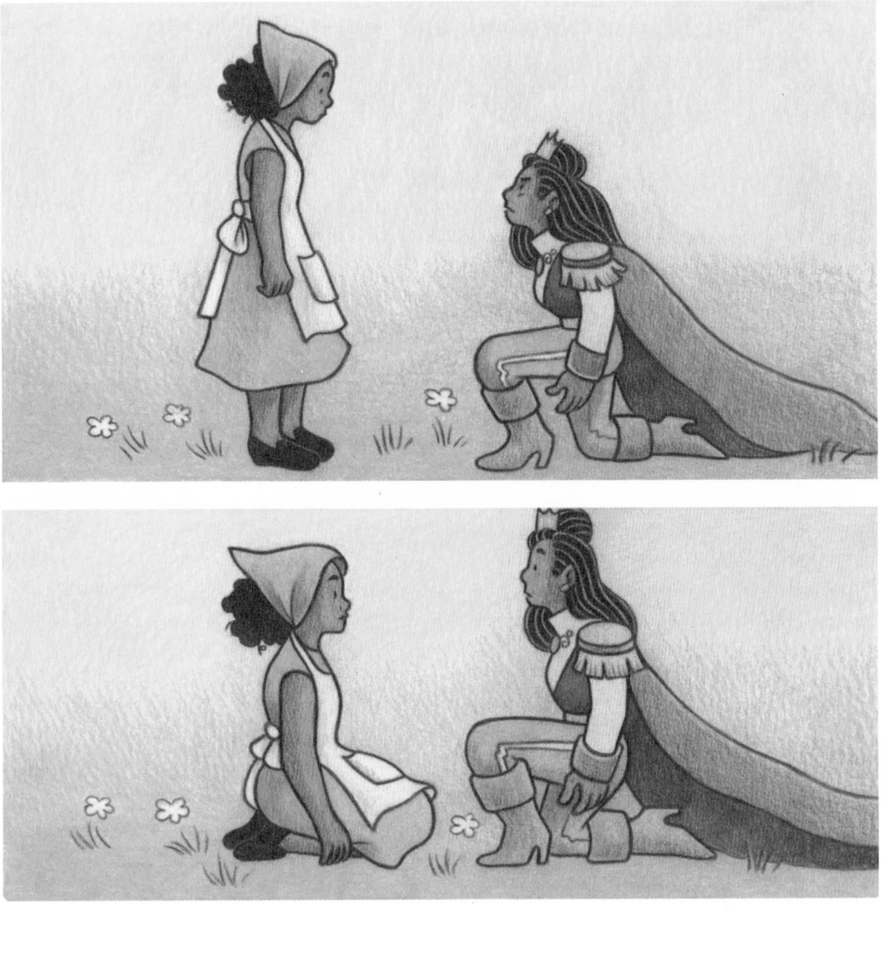

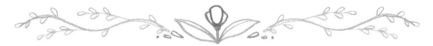

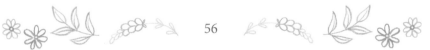

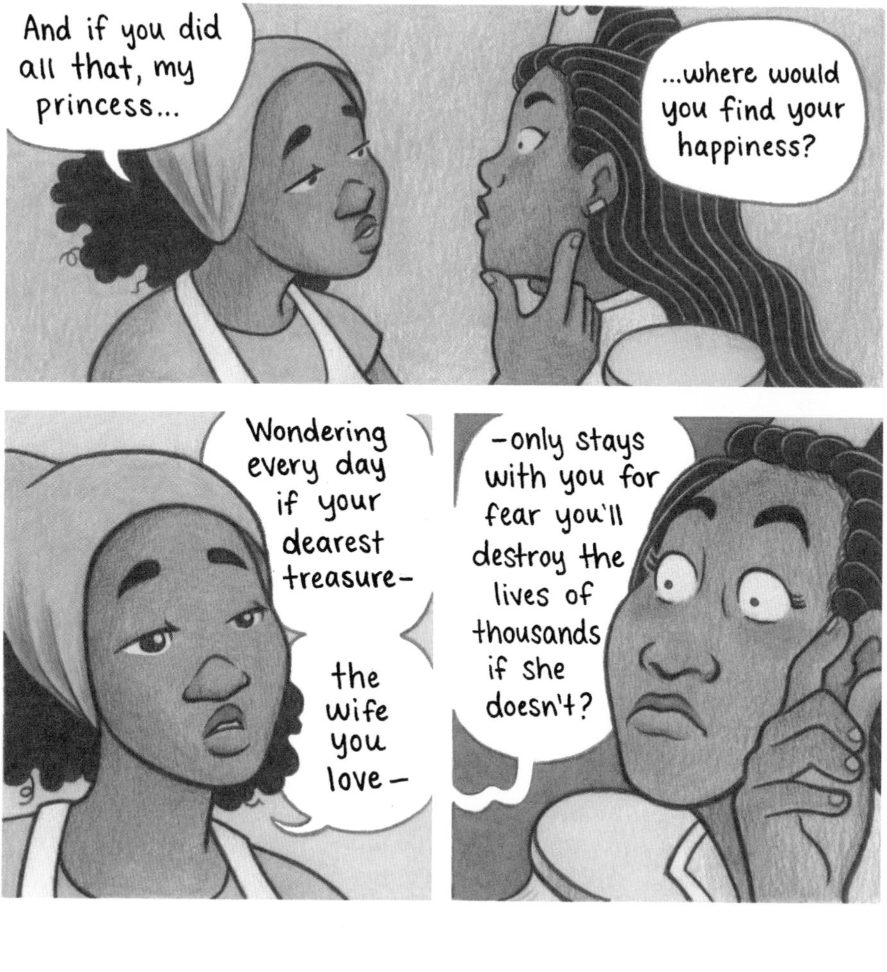
And if you did all that, my princess...
...where would you find your happiness?
Wondering every day if your dearest treasure-
the wife you love-
-only stays with you for fear you'll destroy the lives of thousands if she doesn't?

Do you need help, traveler?
Goose Girl.

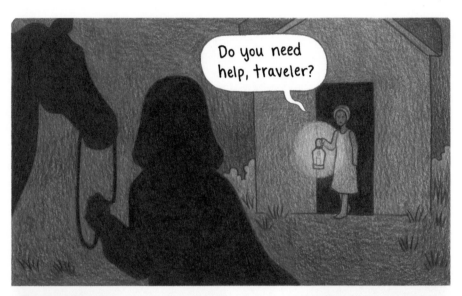

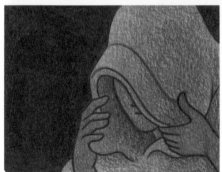

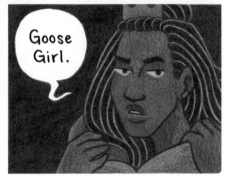

This is the
key to the
royal treasury.

I am going into the woods— alone.

If complete happiness is impossible to achieve in the life of a Princess...

...then maybe it's time to try a different sort of life.

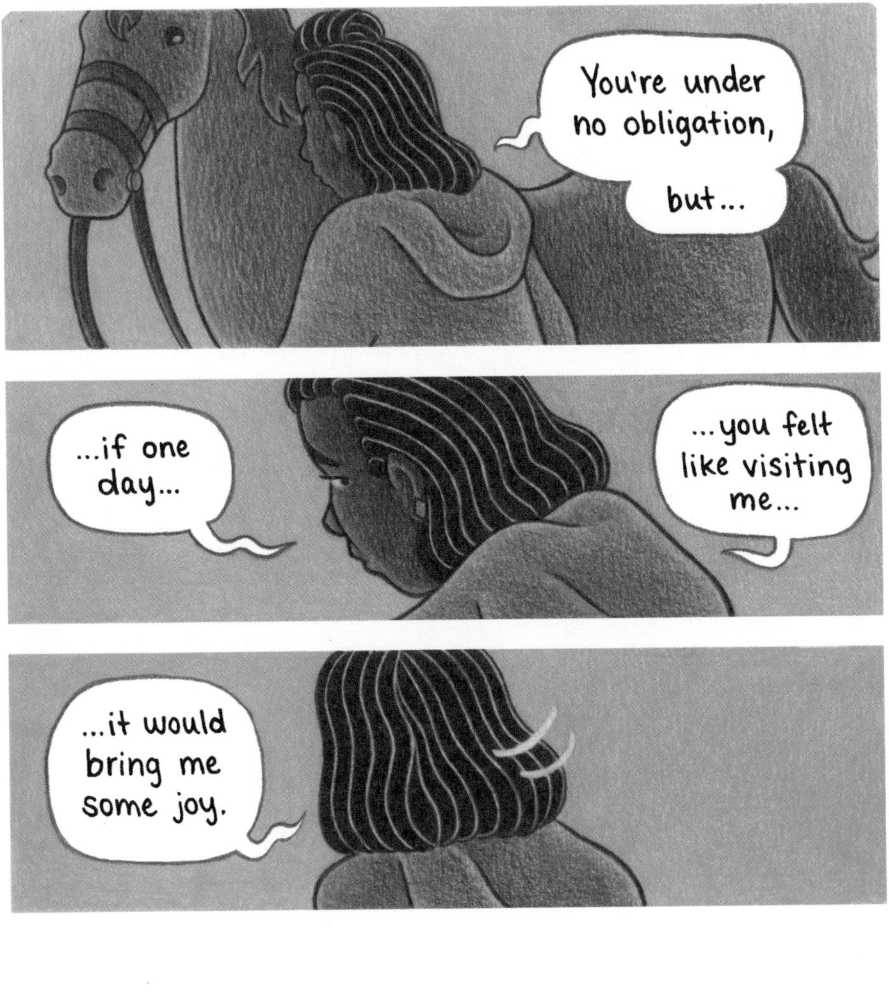
You're under no obligation,
but...
...if one day...
...you felt like visiting me...
...it would bring me some joy.

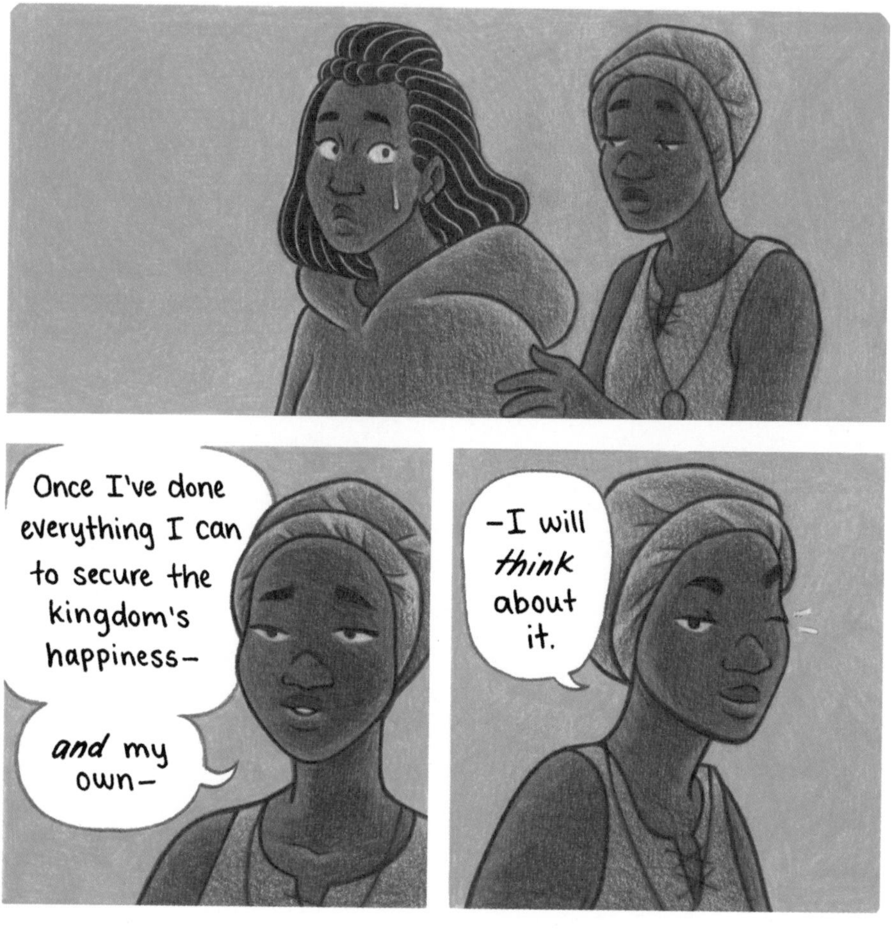
Once I've done everything I can to secure the kingdom's happiness—
and my own—
—I will *think* about it.

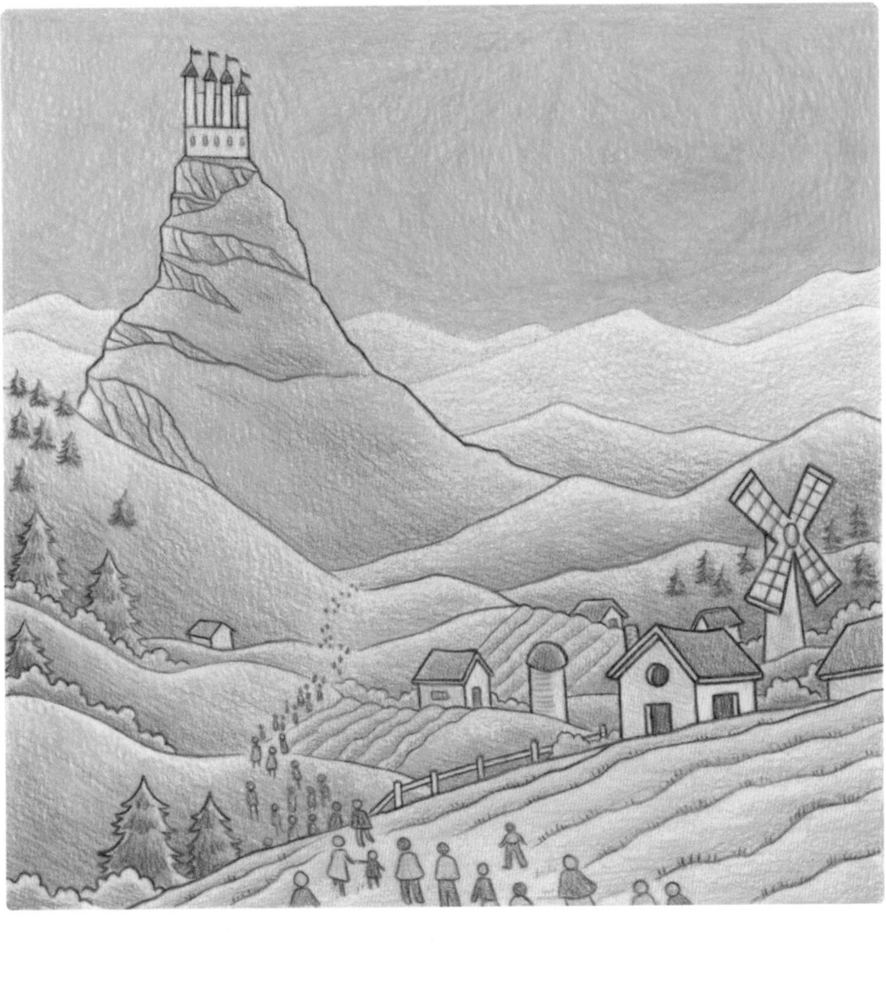

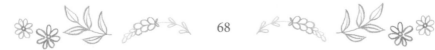

NEW NAME

When I turned ten, I asked my grandmother — the town witch — for a new name.

She agreed, but with a warning.

When you take a new name, the old one can become a powerful tool to harm you.

So the old name must be burned.

Every memory of it.

We set out at once.

Leaving behind my grandfather, patching a leak on our roof.

We went door-to-door.

All over the village.

One by one, everyone who ever knew me,

spoke my name into a magicked pyre.

And bit by bit,
it
burned.

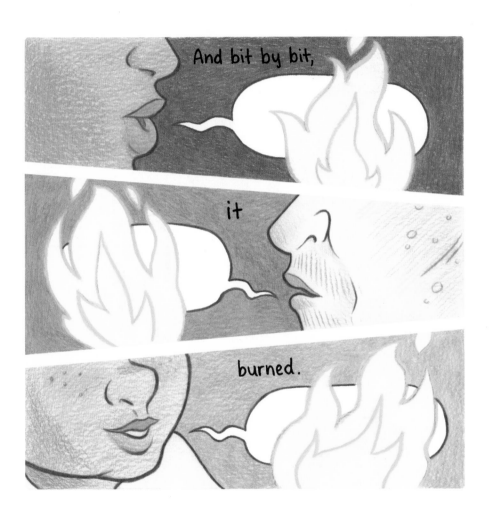

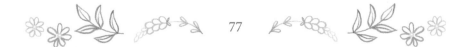

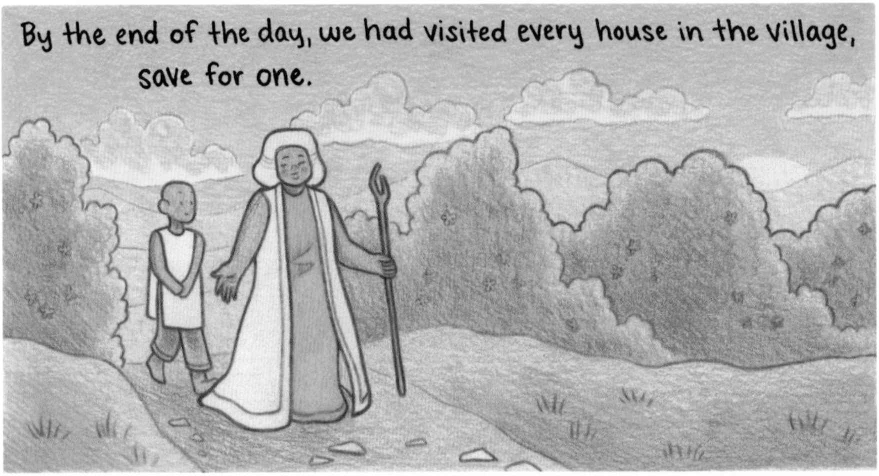
By the end of the day, we had visited every house in the village,
save for one.

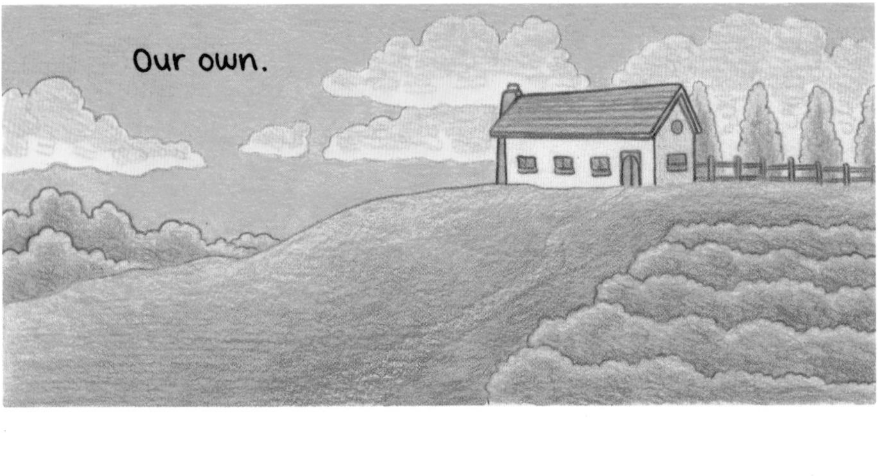
Our own.

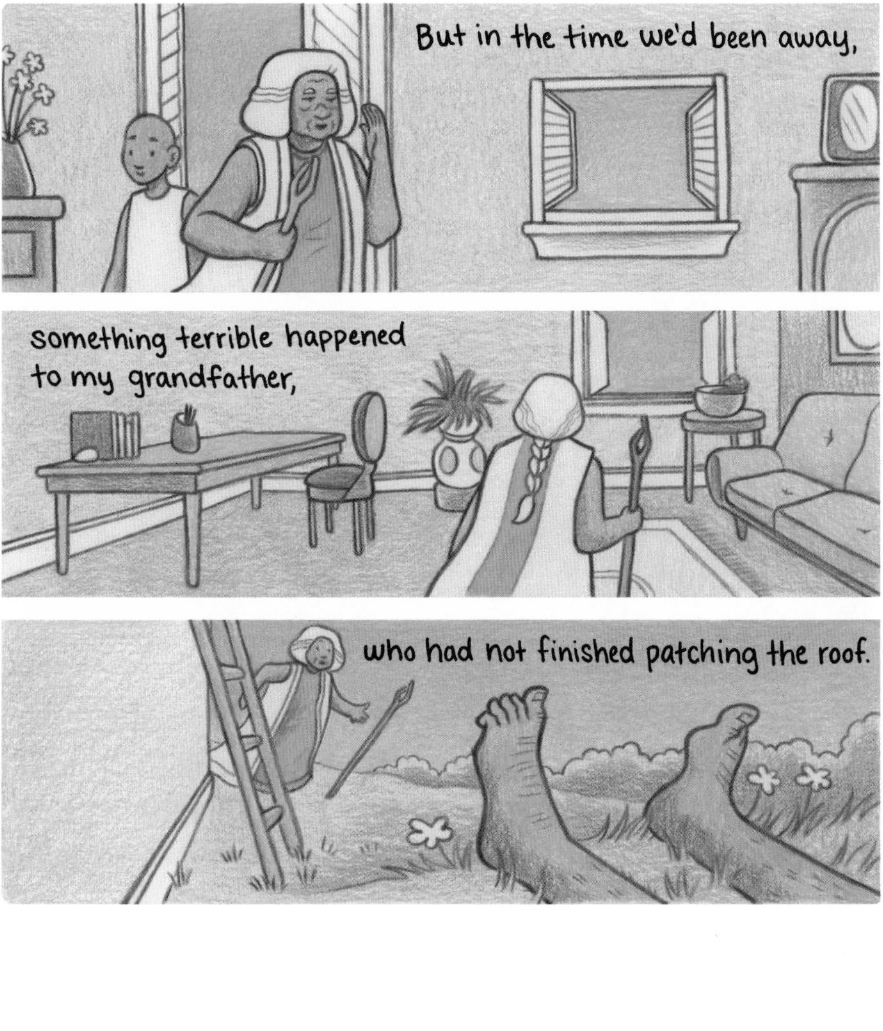
But in the time we'd been away,
something terrible happened to my grandfather,
who had not finished patching the roof.

My grandfather was given his own
pyre the next day.

Never having
heard my
new name.

He did not
stay there,
though.

WHERE IS MY GRANDCHILD?

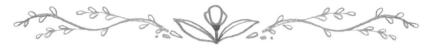

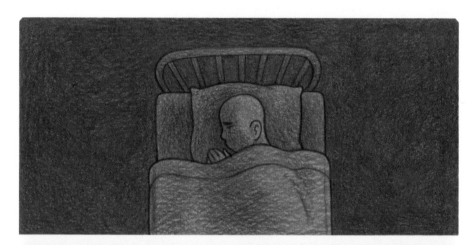

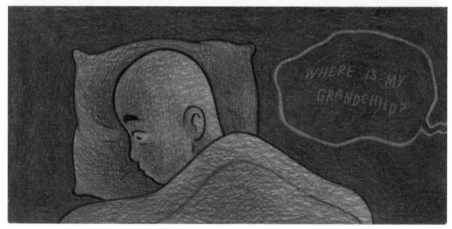

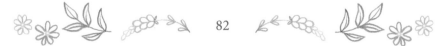

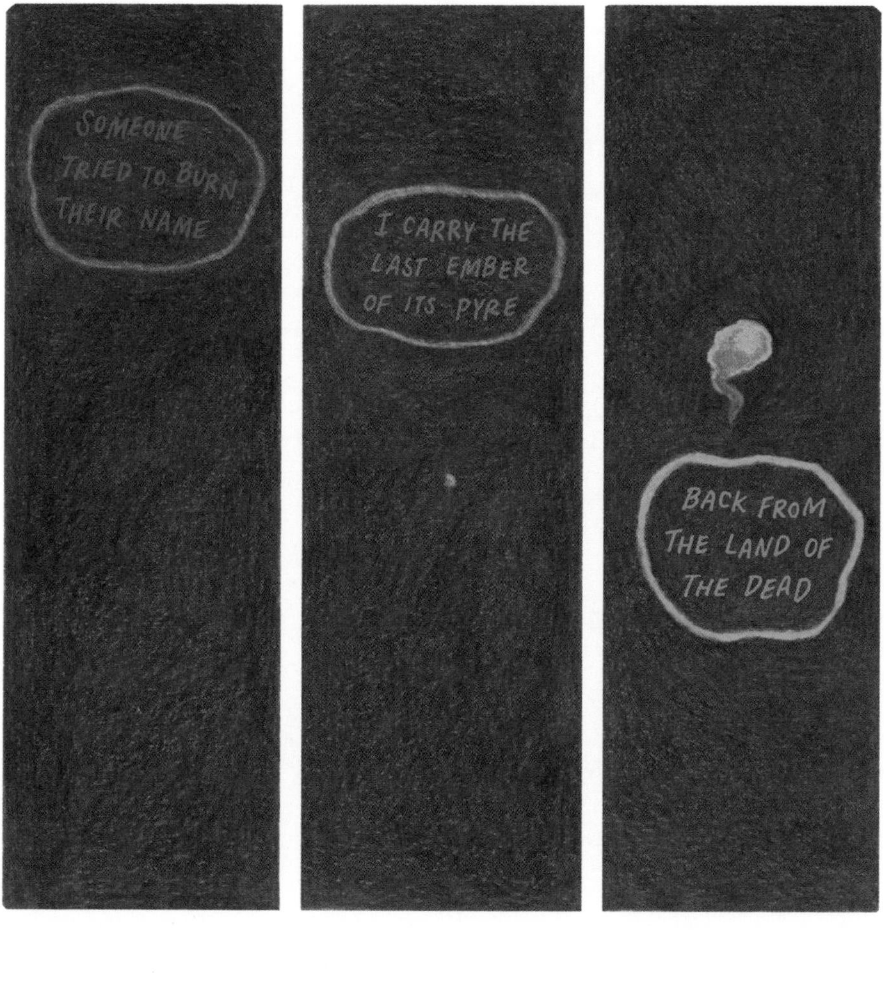
SOMEONE TRIED TO BURN THEIR NAME
I CARRY THE LAST EMBER OF ITS PYRE
BACK FROM THE LAND OF THE DEAD

TO REVIVE IT

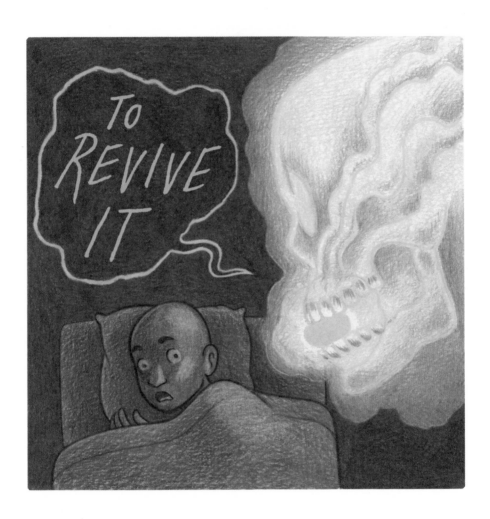

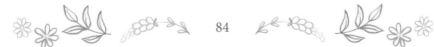

No one else saw him.

No one else heard him.

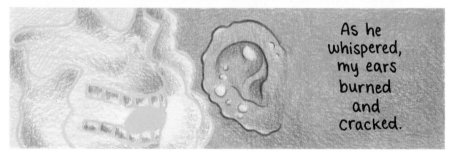

As he whispered, my ears burned and cracked.

I knew I should tell my grandmother.
It's so quiet...

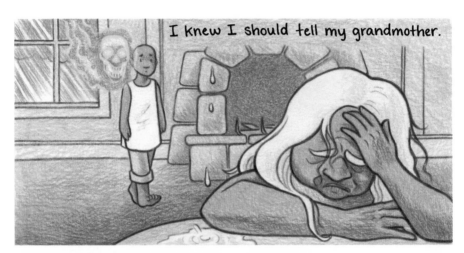

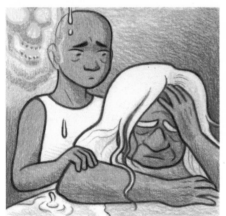

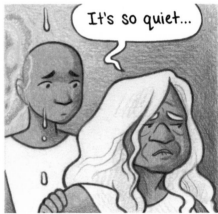

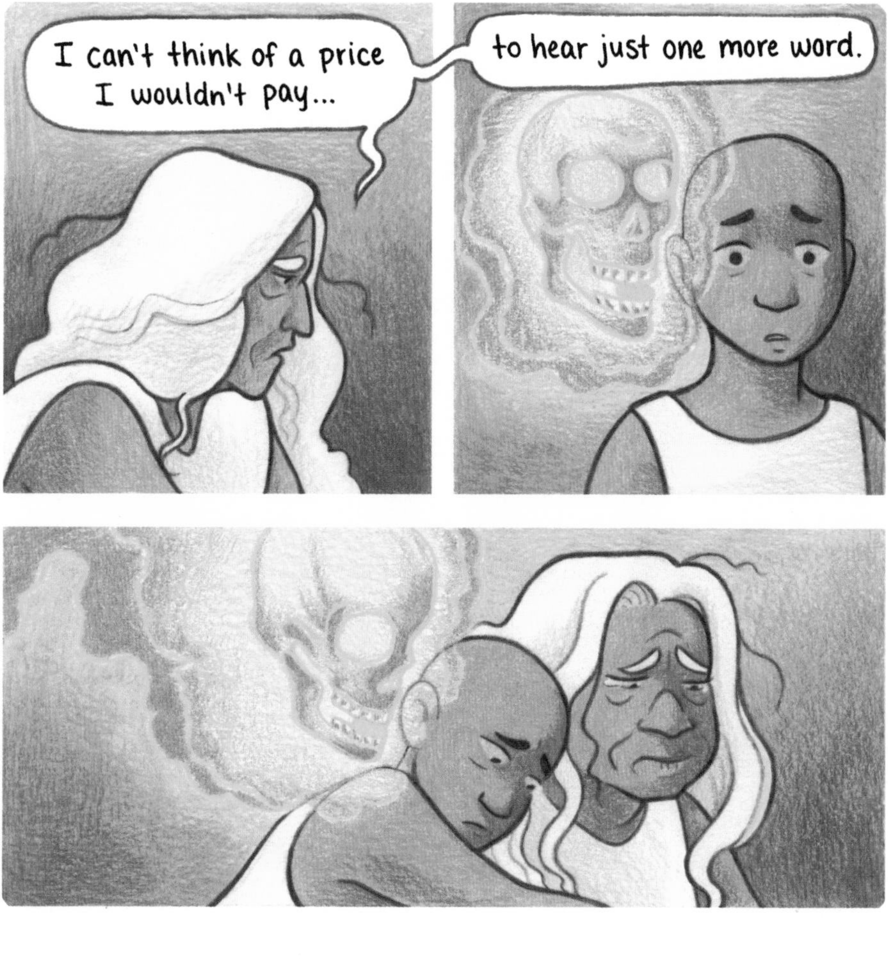
I can't think of a price I wouldn't pay...
to hear just one more word.

I told myself I could wait a little longer.

I carried on, saying nothing.

And within a week, my ears were black.

Finally, once the pain was too much to bear,

I crept out of the house.

Back to my grandfather's pyre.

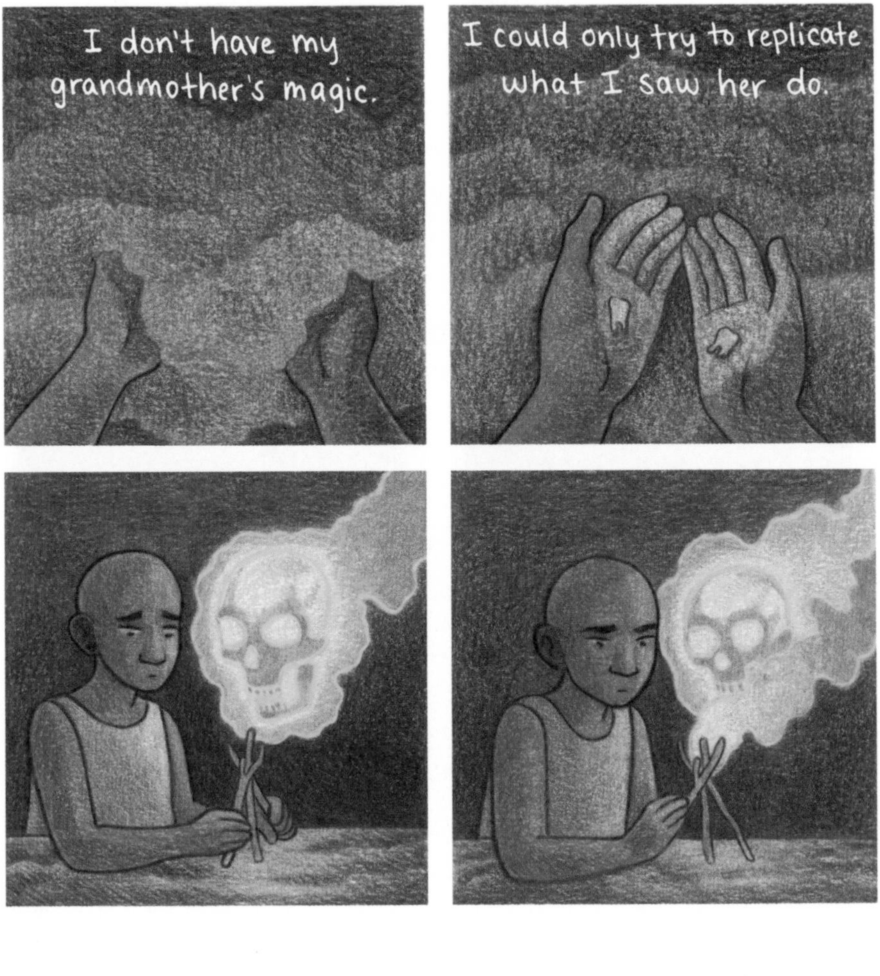
I don't have my grandmother's magic.
I could only try to replicate what I saw her do.

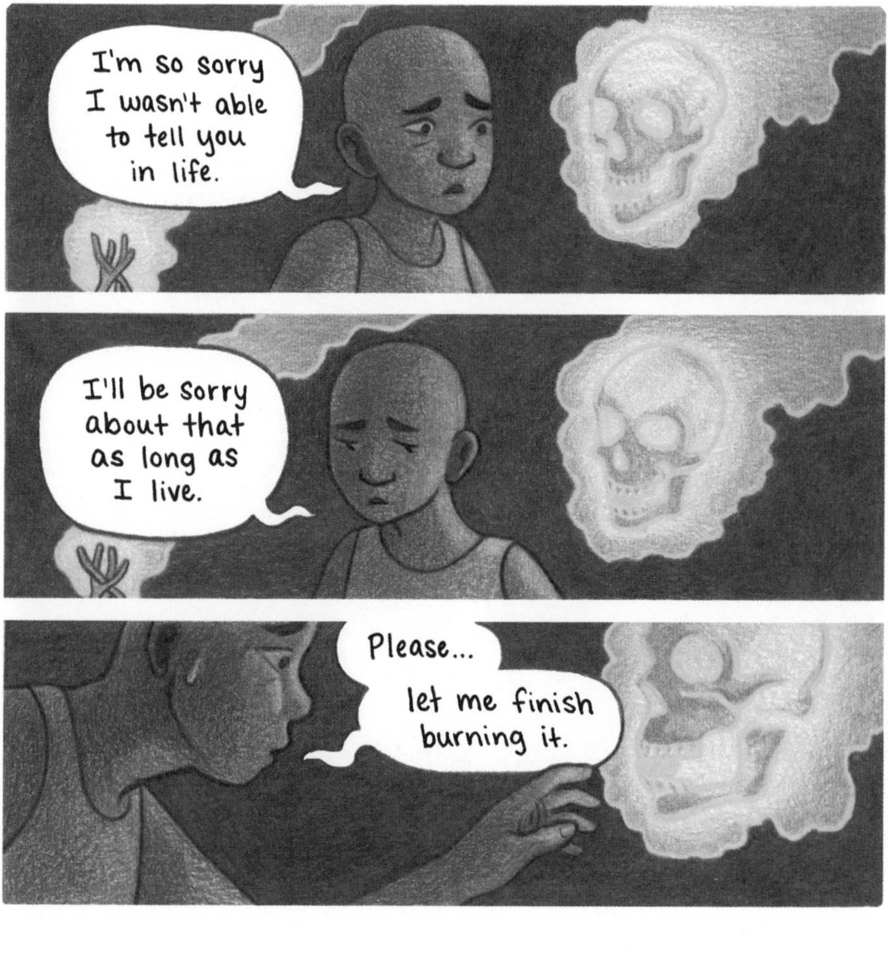
I'm so sorry I wasn't able to tell you in life.
I'll be sorry about that as long as I live.
Please...
let me finish burning it.

WHAT ARE YOU DOING?!
PYRES ARE MEANT TO GO OUT!

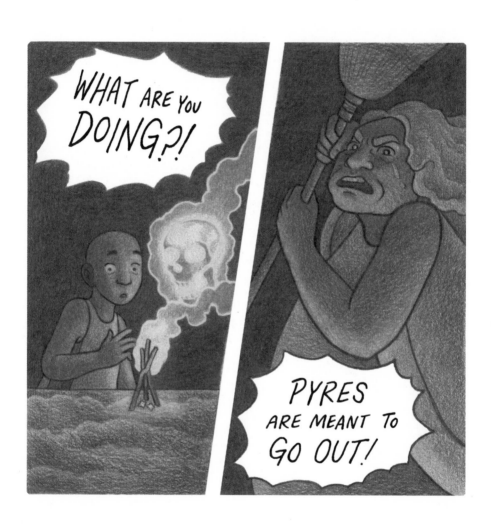

WAIT!

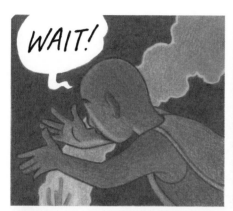

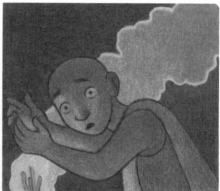

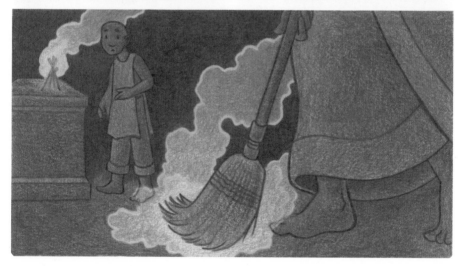

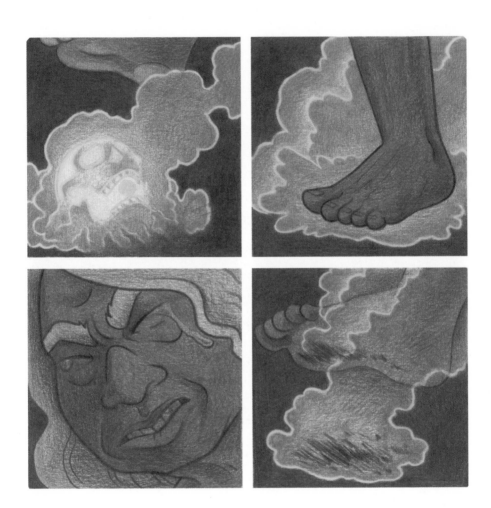

Please—forgive me for not seeing it sooner.

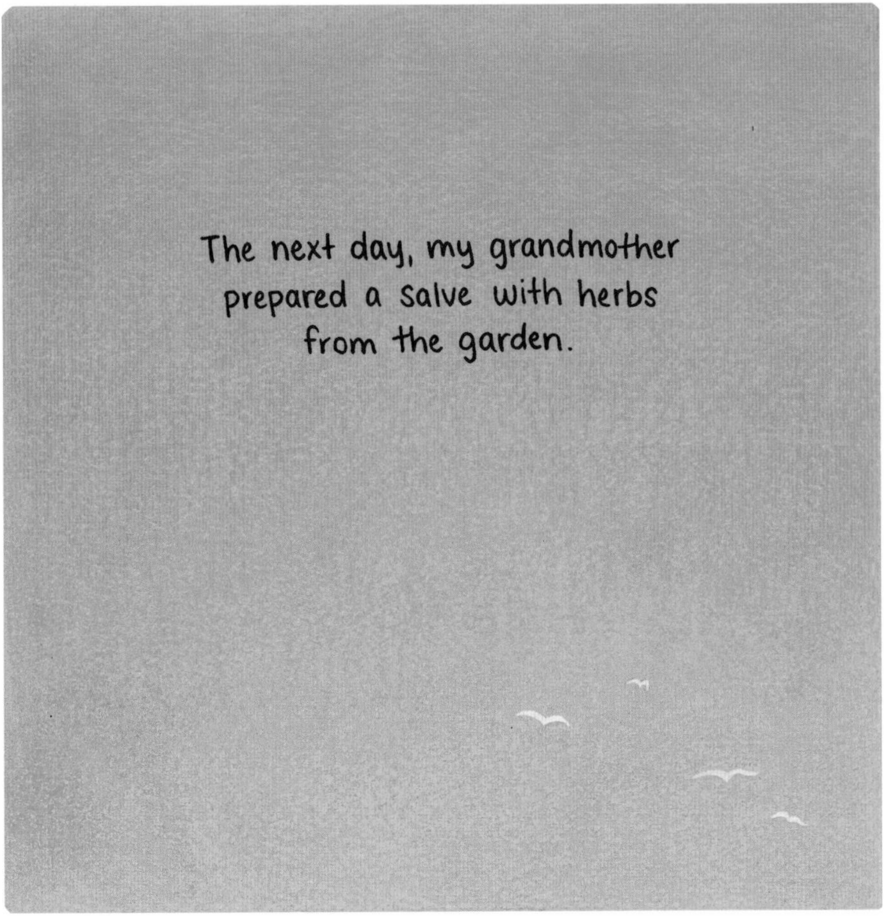

The next day, my grandmother
prepared a salve with herbs
from the garden.

We went door-to-door once again.

One by one, my neighbors all spoke my new name into the salve.

This time, to strengthen it.

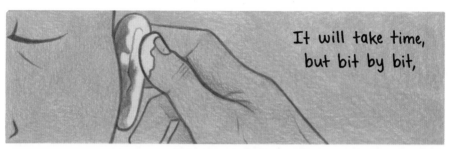

It will take time,
but bit by bit,

we'll heal.

SWEET ROCK

The men in my village believe themselves clever.

Every harvest...

the Giantess in the cavern demands one of our girls to devour.

So every year, we say: "Take any girl you like!

"But please, spare us Eunice the Ugly, or Bertha the Cold, or Margaret the Barren— for she is _far_ too dear to us!"

And thus, every year, which girl does she insist upon?

EUNICE THE UGLY   BERTHA THE COLD   MARGARET THE BARREN

This year, the Giantess has demanded me.

I am bitter, I am told.

On my last day, I crush dry, sour herbs between my teeth.

That I may taste as unyielding as the winter cold.

The Giantess is too big to see all at once.

Just an eye,

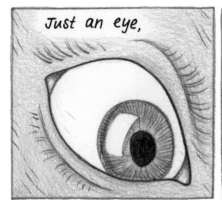

a signet ring,

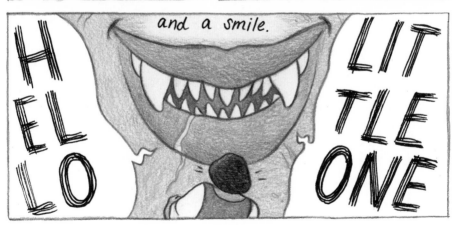

and a smile.

HE LLO

LIT TLE ONE

WE HAVE A LONG JOURNEY; YOU MAY RIDE MY SHOULDER
You... are not going to devour me immediately?
DO YOU WISH ME TO?
YOU HUMANS HAVE SO MANY FIDDLY BONES
I WILL NEED A TOOTHPICK FIRST

AH, THIS WILL DO

THOUGH, PERHAPS, IF YOU SING FOR ME, I MAY SPARE YOU A DAY

I am told my voice is weak—

THE CAVERN MAY LEND ITS OWN VOICE, IF YOU PLEASE IT...

"...Fare ye well, my mother dear, farewell to barn and byre-
And fare ye well, the bonny lass who kindles my mother's fire..."
"I wish the wind may never cease- nor fashes in the flood..."
"TILL MY TRUE LOVE COME HOME TO ME-
-IN EARTHLY FLESH AND BLOOD-"

We continued as such for many days.

IF YOU PULL IT, PERHAPS I WILL SPARE YOU A DAY....
IF YOU MEND IT....
IF YOU SCRATCH IT....
IF YOU SOOTHE IT ...

Nothing about her can rightly be called a small detail—

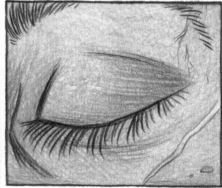

and yet, it is the small details that transfix me.

Her fingers can crush stone,

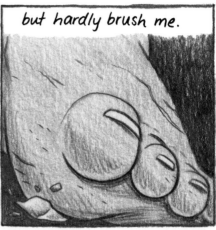

but hardly brush me.

Others before me have clearly dashed their time on her teeth—

but I am kept in suspense.

And after I had long since lost count of days–

IF YOU COLLECT IT...
DRINK–WE NEAR THE END OF OUR JOURNEY
It's...so much sweeter than expected.
I wonder... if it makes me sweeter as well.

HA
HA
HA
HA

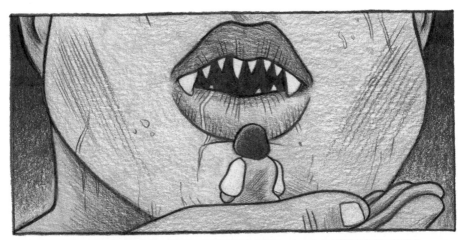

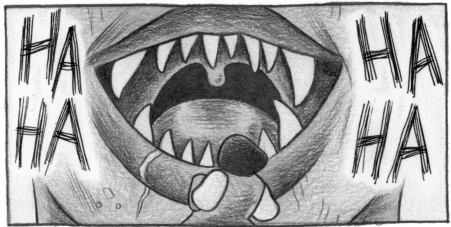

YOU ARE A BOLD MORSEL-
IT IS A SHAME....
YOU
WERE SO
DILIGENT
AT ALL MY
TASKS
WE ARE HERE

Before me, a village I don't recognize.

And all the women—who I do.

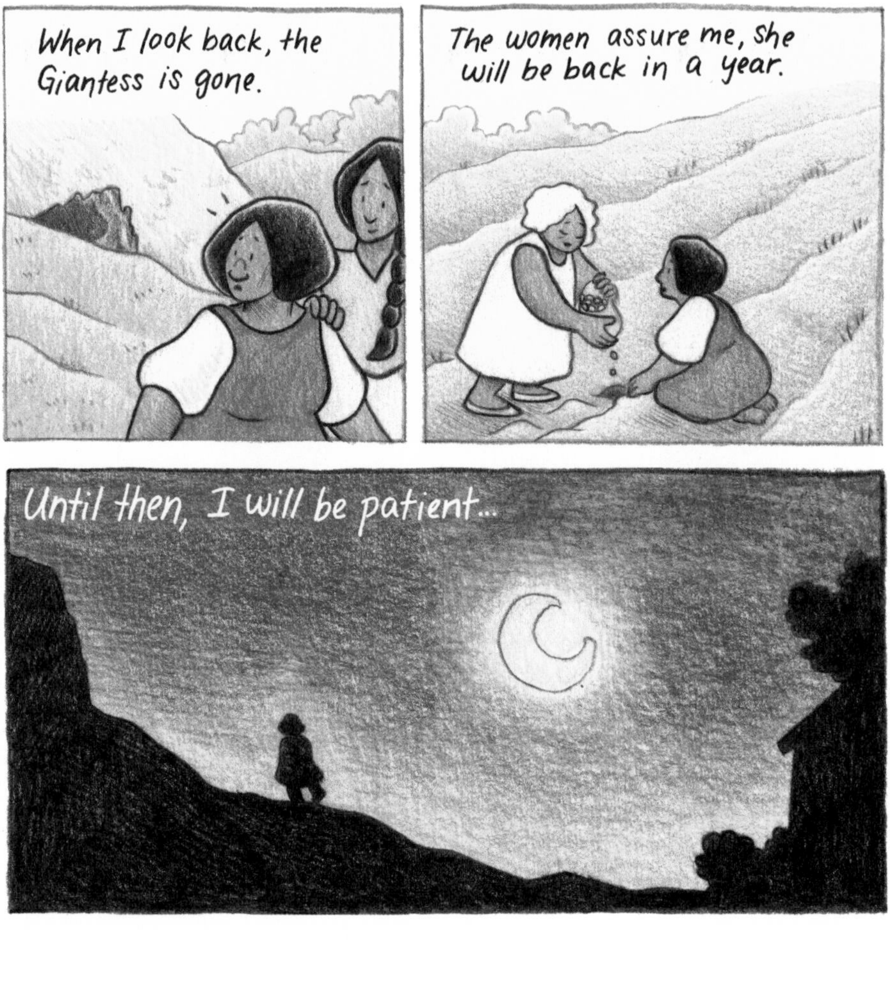
When I look back, the Giantess is gone.
The women assure me, she will be back in a year.
Until then, I will be patient...

and keep myself sweet.

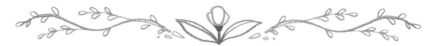

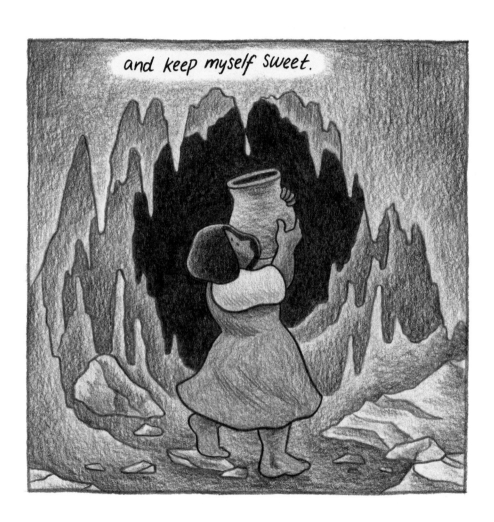

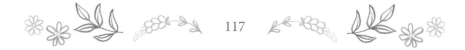

ASTHETE

HSTHETE IS OUR GODDESS OF MISHAPS.

WHENEVER A GLASS IS SPILLED,

OR THE CHICKENS BREAK LOOSE,

OR I SLEEP THROUGH ANOTHER ROOSTER CALL AND GET A SCOLDING,

IT IS SAID THAT SHE IS TO BLAME.

-PTU-

THOUGH SHE TOUCHES OUR LIVES DAILY, NO ONE EVER SEES HER.
I AM LOOKING FOR HER, THOUGH.
BECAUSE I AM IN DESPERATE NEED OF A MISHAP.

SURELY SHE MUST WANT, EVERY ONCE IN A WHILE, TO BE SEEN?
RRRIPPP
Wait-!

STOP!
PLEASE!
I NEED YOUR HELP!

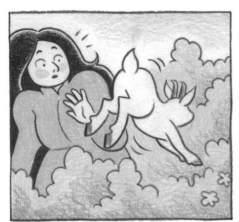

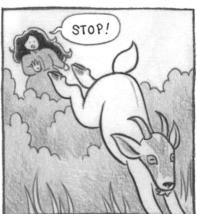

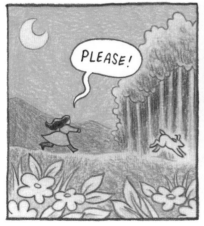

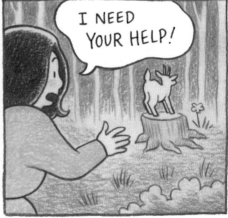

With WHAT, mortal?
I need a mishap to end my betrothal.
Please.

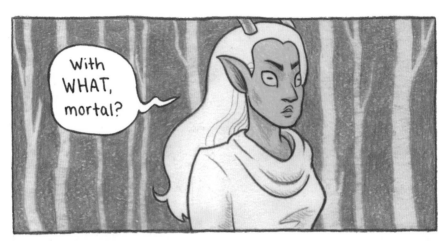

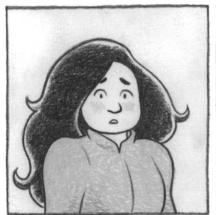

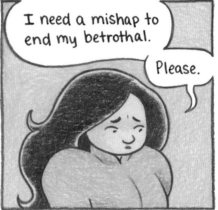

Your fiancé — I've seen him.

He is tall and handsome,

with a manor by the sea?

Yes.

And he is kind, beloved by many, chosen specifically for you by your parents?

Yes.

Then surely there can be no objection to such a man?

No, but—

Not once, in all the times he has visited me—

—has he ever *looked* at me.

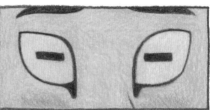

Then take my comb.

—he will be unable to look away.

It will make your hair so lustrous—

THE NEXT DAY, ALL THE MILK IN THE HOUSE CURDLED.

THE CAT DESTROYED OUR BEST TABLECLOTH.

AND ALL DAY, I WORE THE COMB.

BUT MY TALL, KIND, BELOVED FIANCÉ STILL DID NOT LOOK AT ME ONCE.

THE NEXT NIGHT, I BROKE A FAVORITE BOWL IN THE YARD.

Shame to waste the finery, no?

Please, I need a mishap. My wedding is in three days.

Even with your comb—

—he still never looked once.

Then here—
take my bell.

When you laugh, it will ring so beautifully, he will have no choice but to look.

If only to see what brings you such mirth.

THE NEXT DAY, WHENEVER MY FIANCÉ TOLD A JOKE,

I LAUGHED LOUDEST OF ALL.

AND MY RICH, GENEROUS, POPULAR HUSBAND-TO-BE...

STILL DID NOT ONCE TURN HIS HEAD.

SO THAT NIGHT, I DROPPED A LEFT SHOE DOWN THE WELL.

Getting rather accident-prone,
aren't we?
Please, I beg you! My wedding is in two days!
And no amount of laughter will make my fiancé *look at me.*
I have only one thing left to give.

Take my candle.
Use it to light your way home.
And trust me.
On your wedding day, your beloved *will* see you.

I DID AS SHE ASKED.
BUT WITH PRECIOUS LITTLE HOPE.
UP, UP, UP!

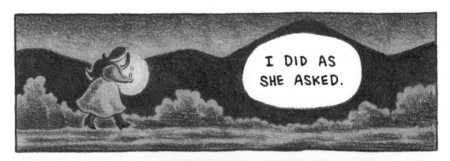

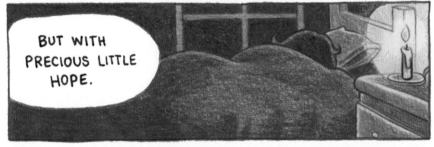

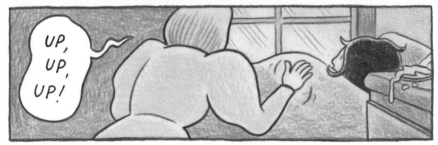

The rooster's crowed *thrice*, and your wedding is *today*.

WHAT?

A big storm is coming tomorrow, so you must be wed *today*.

Your fiancé already sent word he is on his way.

MY WISHED-FOR MISHAP HAD FINALLY ARRIVED.

BUT ONLY TO DOOM ME FASTER.

BUT THEN, FOR THE VERY FIRST TIME,

I FELT...

THE FULL FORCE

OF MY SPOUSE-TO-BE'S GAZE

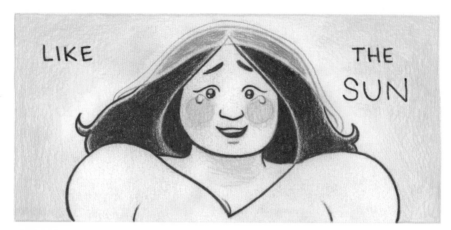

LIKE THE SUN

IT DID INDEED STORM THE NEXT DAY.

MY HANDSOME, RICH, POPULAR BETROTHED WAS QUITE SOAKED THROUGH

BY THE TIME HE ARRIVED AT THE CHURCH.

MEANWHILE, IN A HOME ON A MOUNTAINTOP FAR AWAY,

I SLEPT THROUGH ANOTHER ROOSTER'S CALL.

IF I AM LUCKY, I MAY LIVE TO DO SO MANY, MANY TIMES MORE.

THE FISH WIFE

I wasn't sure if today would be the day I drowned,

but I went down to the dock anyway to decide.

My face in the water

began to change.

I HAVE SEEN YOUR HEART, DEAR ONE.

AND TASTED YOUR TEARS IN MY WATERS THESE FORTY YEARS.

YOUR VILLAGE IS SMALL.
YOU KNOW EVERYONE IN IT, AND NONE CAN LOVE YOU.
BUT *I* CAN LOVE YOU.

FOR ONE YEAR, I WILL BE YOUR WIFE, AND YOU WILL KNOW LOVE.

BUT IF IN A YEAR AND A DAY, YOU STILL LOVE ME,

THEN I WILL ASK YOU FOR YOUR HEART TO FEED TO MY CHILDREN.

I did not drown that day.

We were
married in the
traditional fish way.

And were
very happy
for a time.

The priest railed, and the townswomen stared—

—but for the first time, I do not see or hear them.

In the sun, I see the glimmer of my wife's mica-green hair.

And in the moon, I taste the salt on her skin.

And by the sea, when she laughs,

(for she only laughs by the sea)

I see the pearls in her teeth.

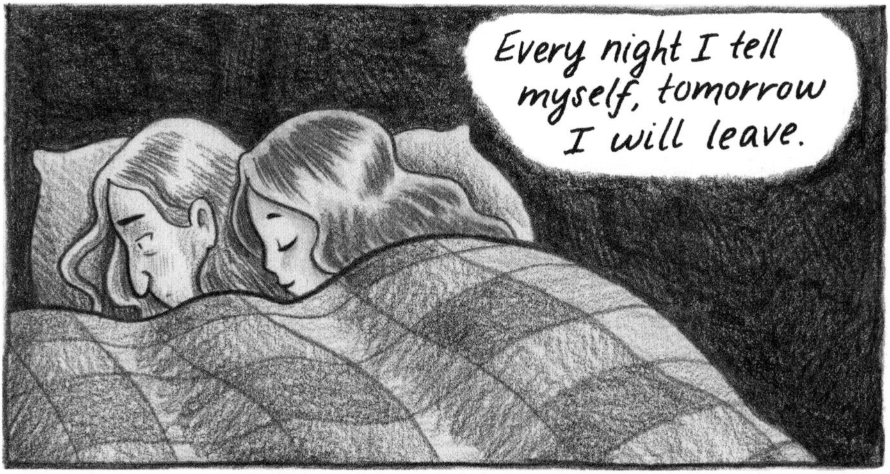
Every night I tell myself, tomorrow I will leave.

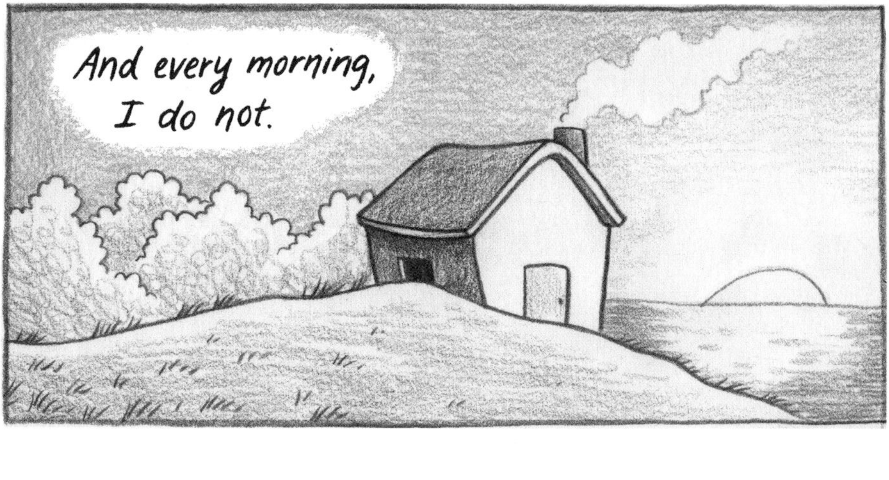
And every morning, I do not.

In the fall, my wife's skin grows cold.

In the winter, when the hearth-fire makes it harder for her to breathe, she grows soft gills.

And I hardly notice when it's spring again.

One day, my wife turns to me and asks—
DEAR ONE, DO YOU LOVE ME STILL?

And to my question in return—
Will your children-?
THEY WILL.

In the water,

where my
wife's mica-
green hair
still glimmers,

and the salt
of her skin
engulfs me,

we meet her
children.

And she introduces me
as "Mother."

THE PEOPLE'S FOREST

As a foundling,
the purpose of my life
has always been clear.

The state saved
my life, so I
owe my life to
the state.

So, from the day I was big enough to hold a sword, I pledged my life in service to the most beautiful girl in the world,

who had herself been given a weighty responsibility.

As she grew as a stateswoman,
I trained to be her sword.
And like a sword,
I found my home at her hilt.

The work was demanding,

but the rewards,

so sweet.

I learned to find pleasure in simple purposes.
To be where I was needed.

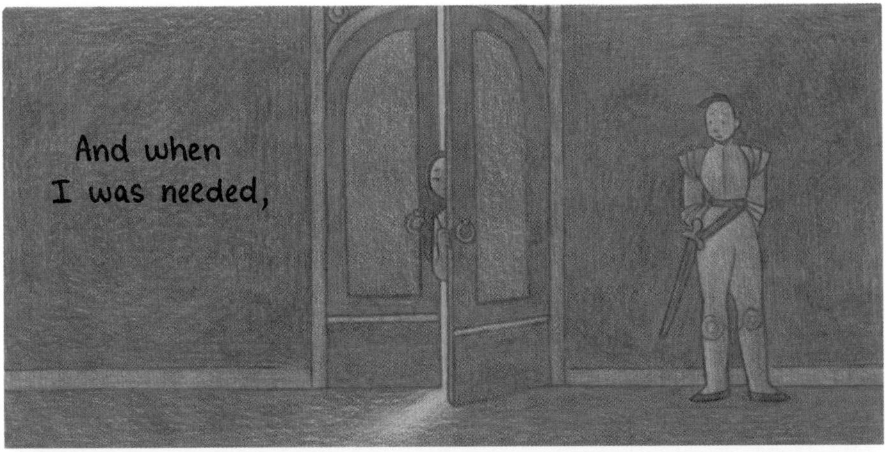
And when
I was needed,

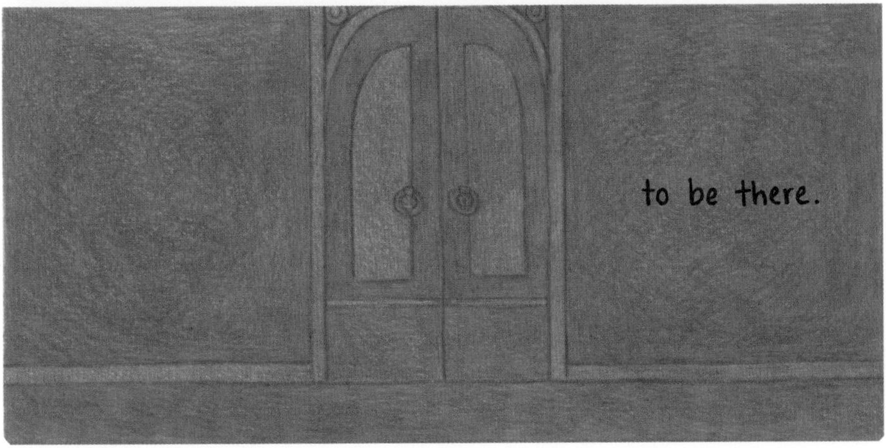
to be there.

I pictured the years of my life strung before me, like so many beads on a string.

Each one a sacrifice,

delicious to make.

Please...
...don't.

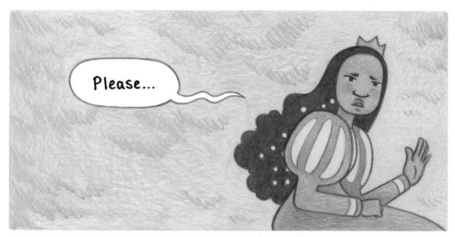

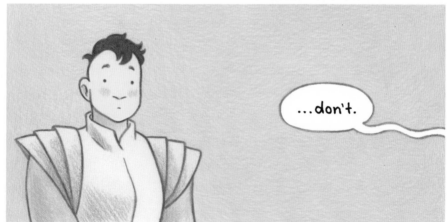

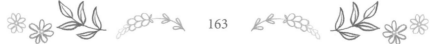

I must marry for state soon.

I've shirked that duty for far too long already.

Suitors arrive every day and I...can barely look at them.

Knowing you're standing behind me, just feet away, as always.

That doesn't bother me.
I'd never come between you and your duties.
I'll come when I'm called and step aside when I'm not-
just like always.

If only I trusted myself to do the same.

As one last act of fidelity, I was asked to leave.

And my greatest joy is to serve.

For one month, I followed rows of young, ripening wheat.

Determined to replace what I'd lost.

Till I reached a kingdom in a valley.

I'd hoped I'd be able

to pledge my services anew.

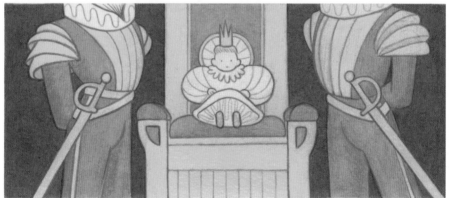

But did not see the thing I sought.

I rode out again.

The next month, I found orderly rows of potatoes.

And climbed up acres of terraces.

I paid my respects
to the Sovereign.

But could not see a place
for myself there, either.

The road grew
wilder as I traveled.

And the nights,
colder.

One day, I followed the smell of sweet, ripe apples.

And found myself in an orchard.

Excuse me – what direction would I ride to find the lord or lady of this place?

This place has no lord or lady!

Whoever you swear allegiance to, I mean?

Only the people you see here.
We haven't had a ruler in some years.
Ah.
I'll be off, then.
Wait!

Winter will be here soon.
If you don't find what you're looking for—
—we can make a place for you here.
...I must make haste, then.

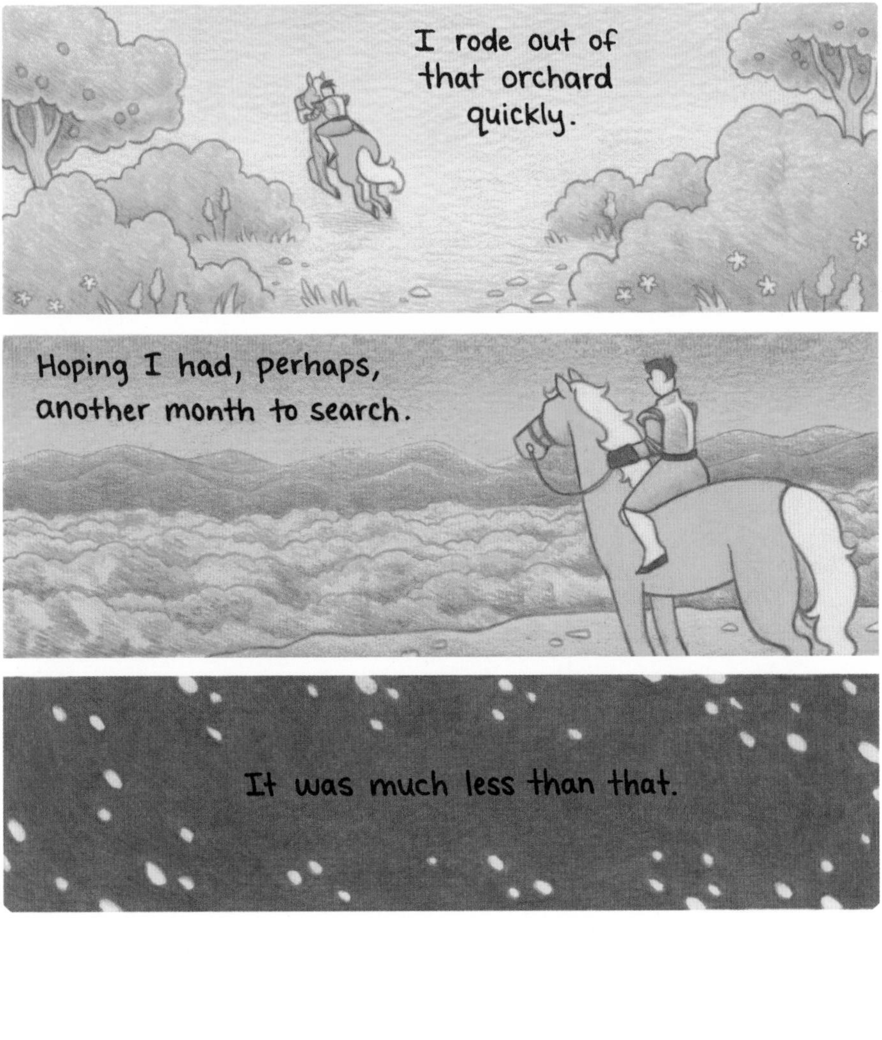
I rode out of
that orchard
quickly.
Hoping I had, perhaps,
another month to search.
It was much less than that.

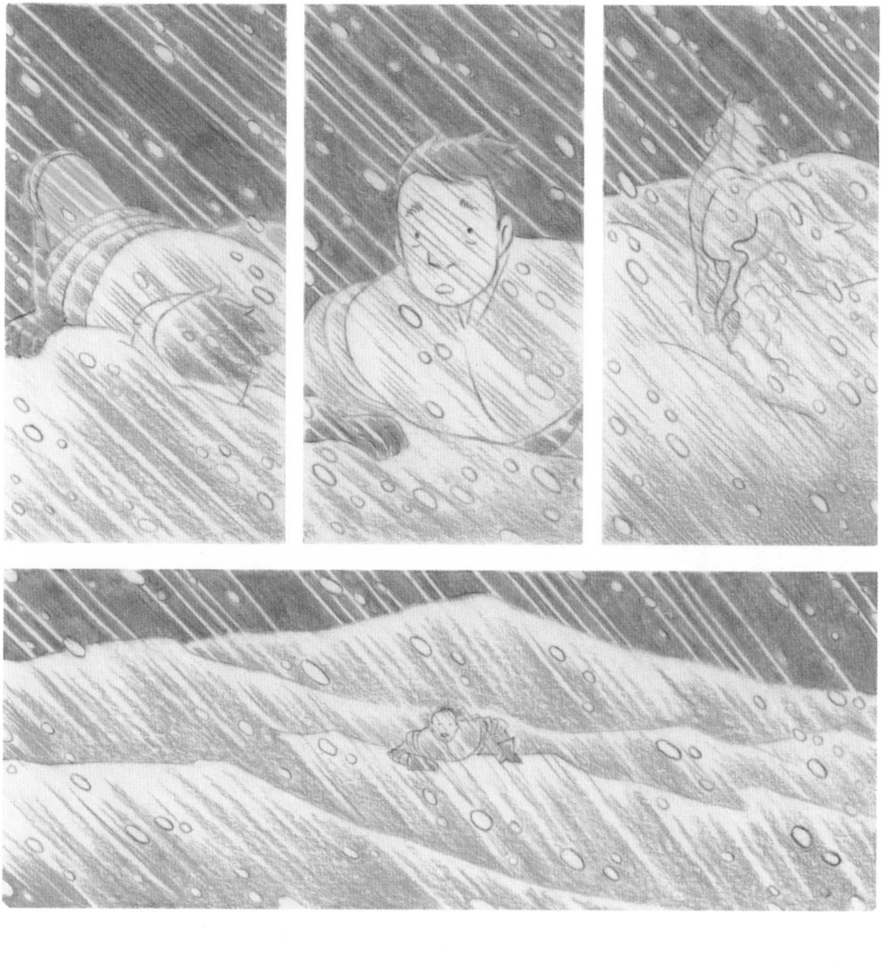

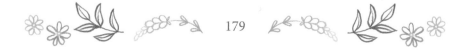

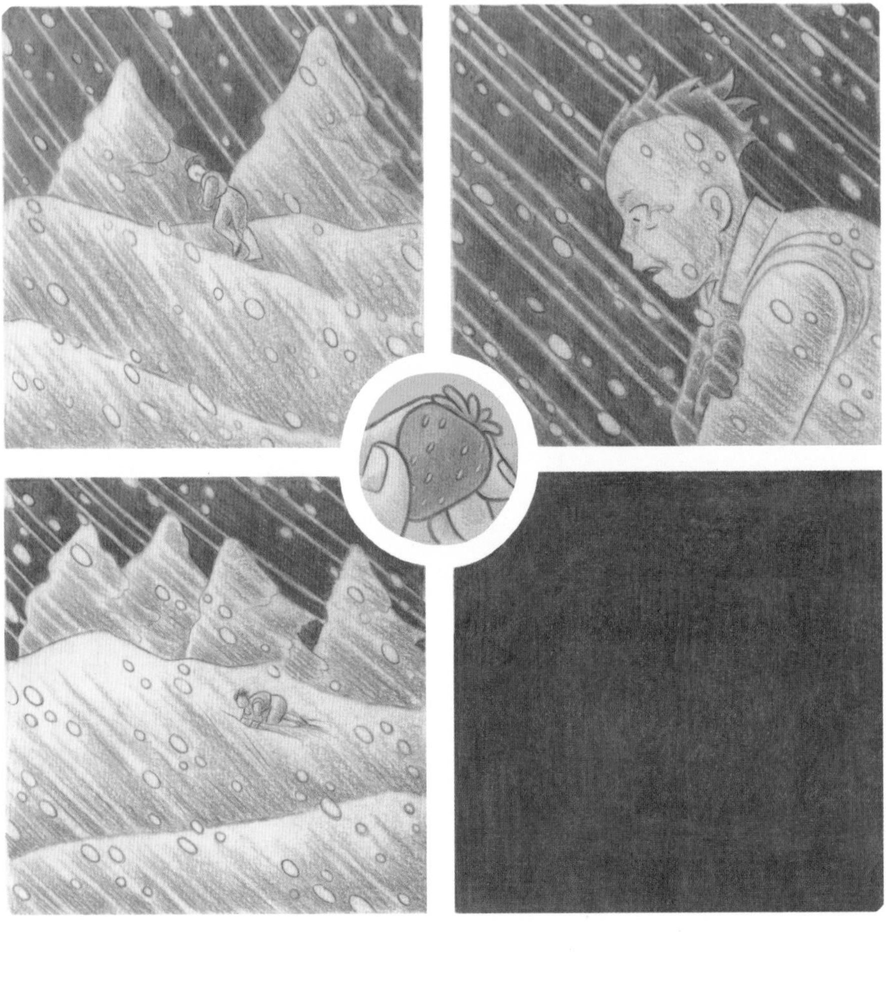

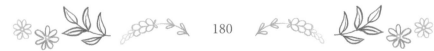

KOFF
KOFF
Shh. Lie back.

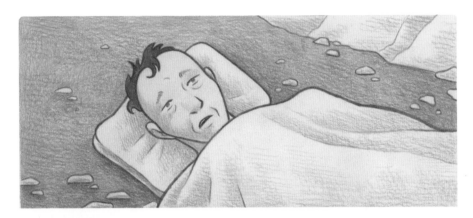

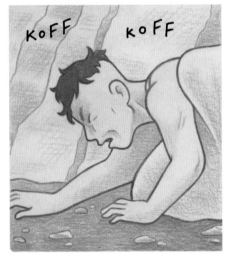

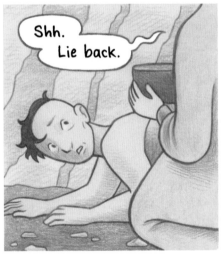

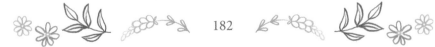

Soup.

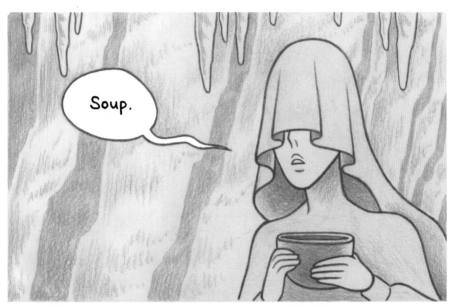

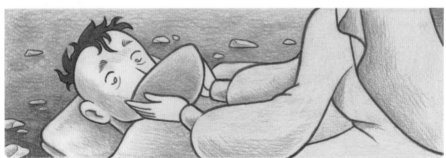

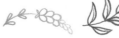

You...
saved me?

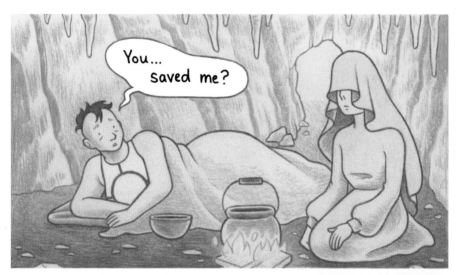

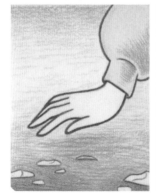

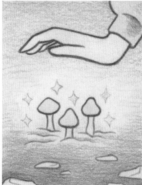

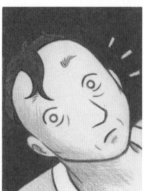

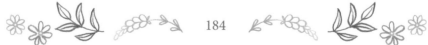

Please–
KoFF
KF
KOFF
KF
Let me repay you!
I will pledge my life in service to you!

No.
Finish the soup.
I've been searching for *months* for someone to serve!
It's all I want!
It's... the only way I'll heal.

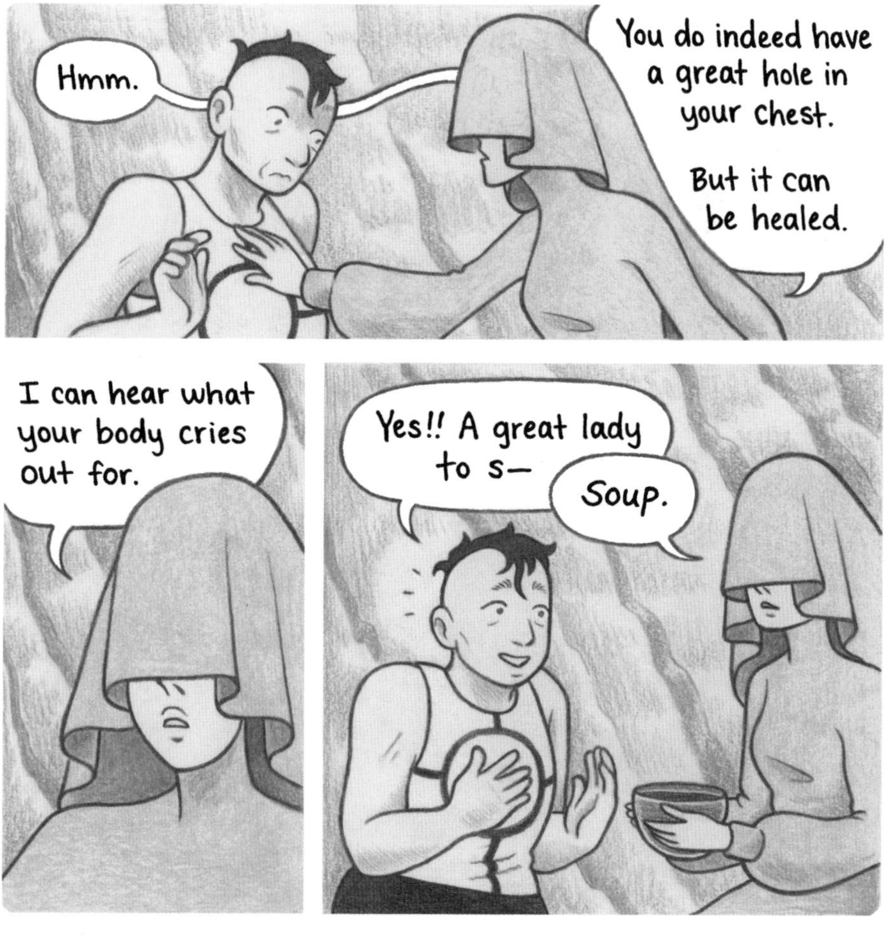
Hmm.
You do indeed have a great hole in your chest.
But it can be healed.
I can hear what your body cries out for.
Yes!! A great lady to s—
Soup.

It was three weeks of soup before I could walk again.

Every day she would leave the cave, and I would try to follow.

When that failed, I'd try something smaller — like picking up my sword.

And when that failed —

Every night, she returned to feed me.
Please!! Accept my vow of service—
No. Eat.
What is the POINT of saving my life if I can't REPAY you??
Eat.

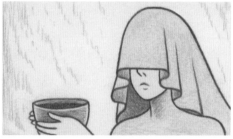

One day, I managed to reach a fallen branch at the mouth of the cave.

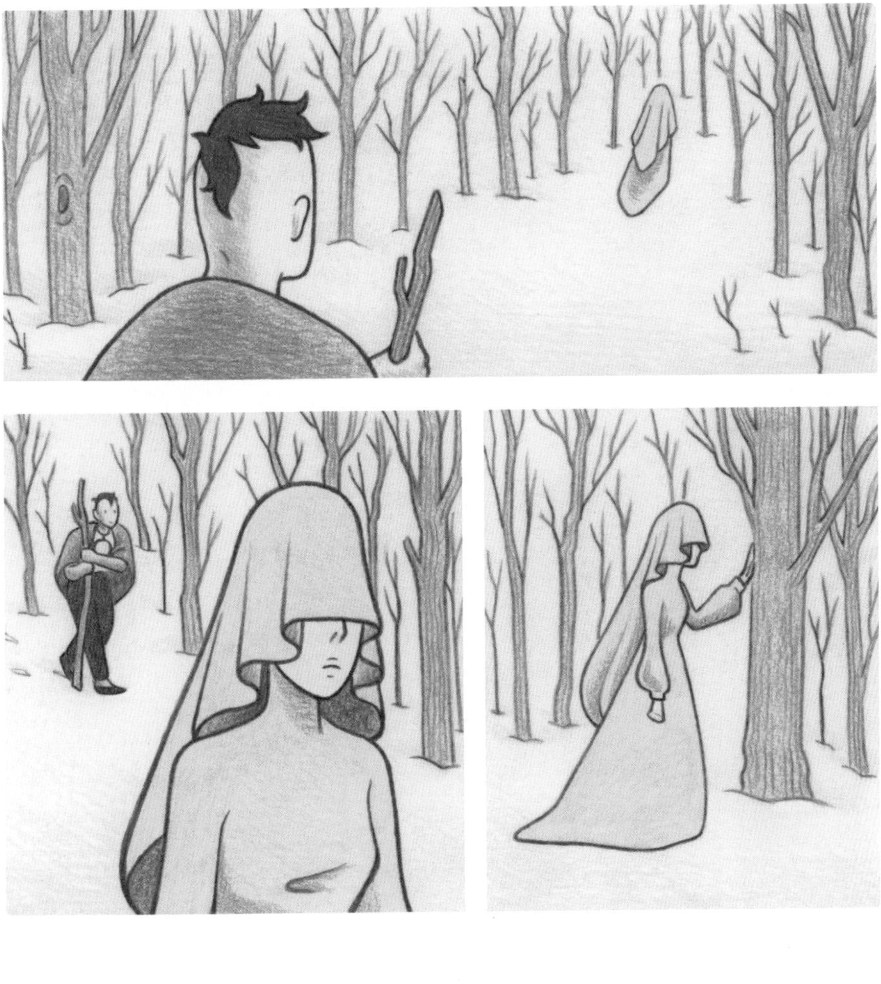

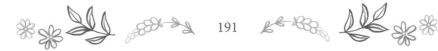

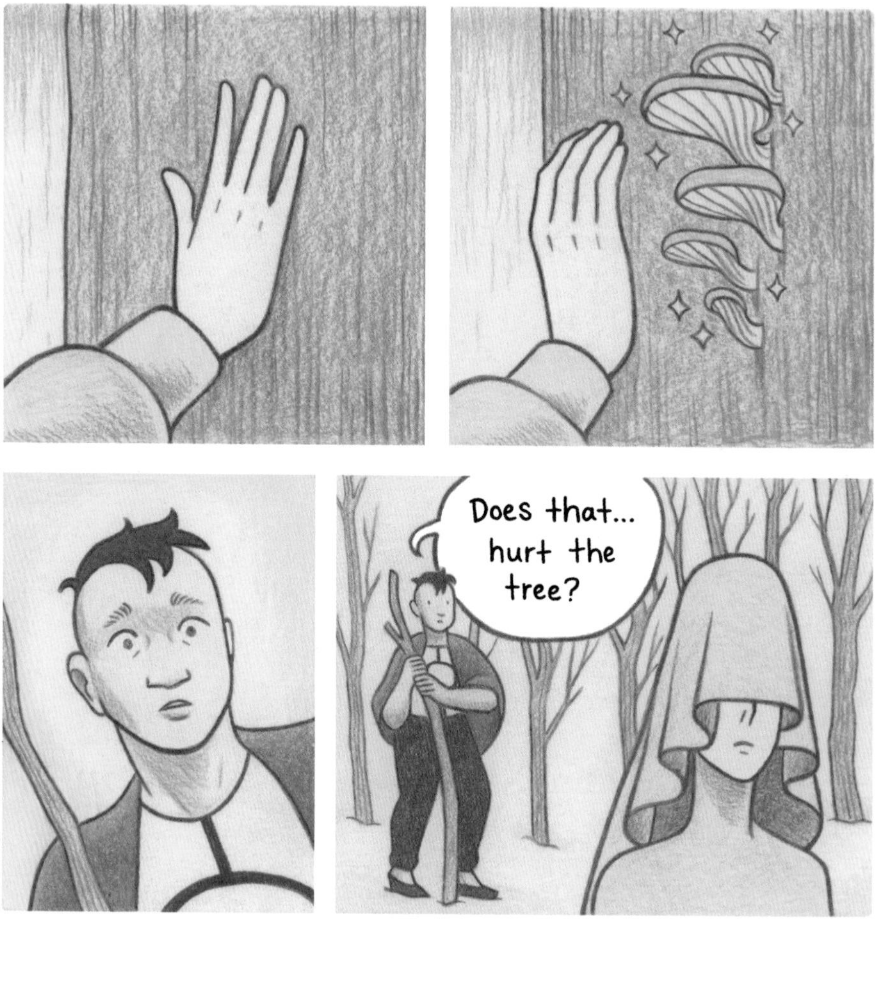
Does that...
hurt the
tree?

It brings it joy.

Below ground, the fungi is a living heart connecting every tree in the forest.
No tree could survive without it.

In gratitude, the tree gives the fungi a gift in return—

—a home to grow and thrive.

Together, each life is strengthened and enriched by the other.

I understand now!

What is given must be repaid!
Through service and sacrifice, they prove their love!

A life spent enriching and strengthening another is my deepest wish as well!

You're hungry again.
I will make soup.

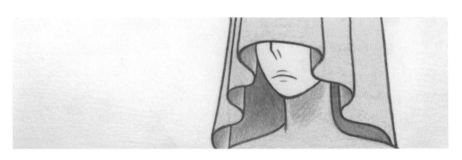

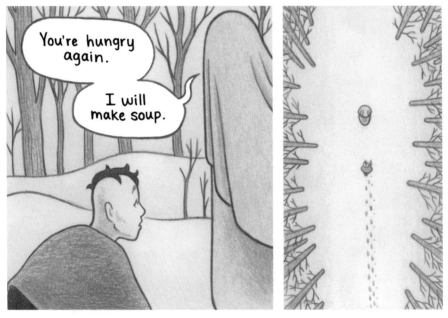

The coming weeks
brought slow changes.

The sun hung in the sky
a few breaths longer.

Bird calls peppered
the cracking of ice.

And my body
remembered
some of
its old
strength.

But the same passage of time seemed to be having the opposite effect on her.

She never mentioned it — and I didn't dare ask —

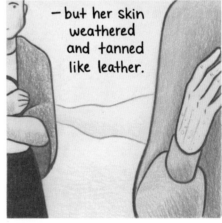

— but her skin weathered and tanned like leather.

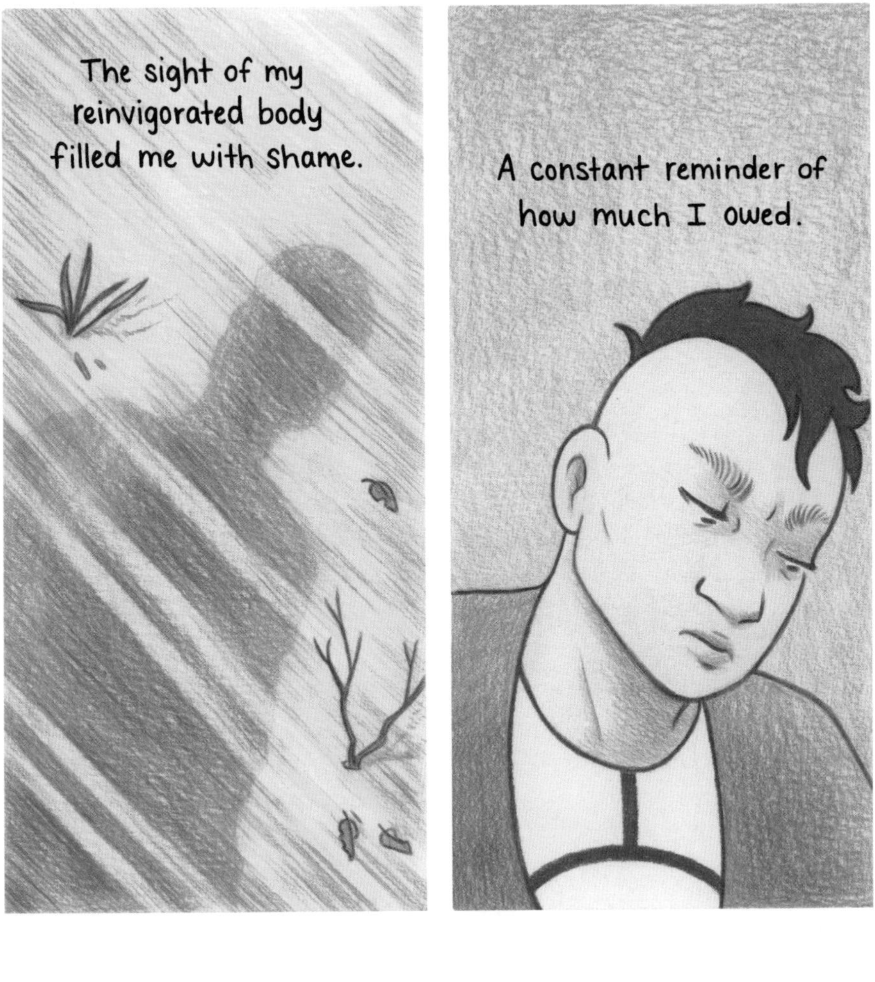
The sight of my
reinvigorated body
filled me with shame.
A constant reminder of
how much I owed.

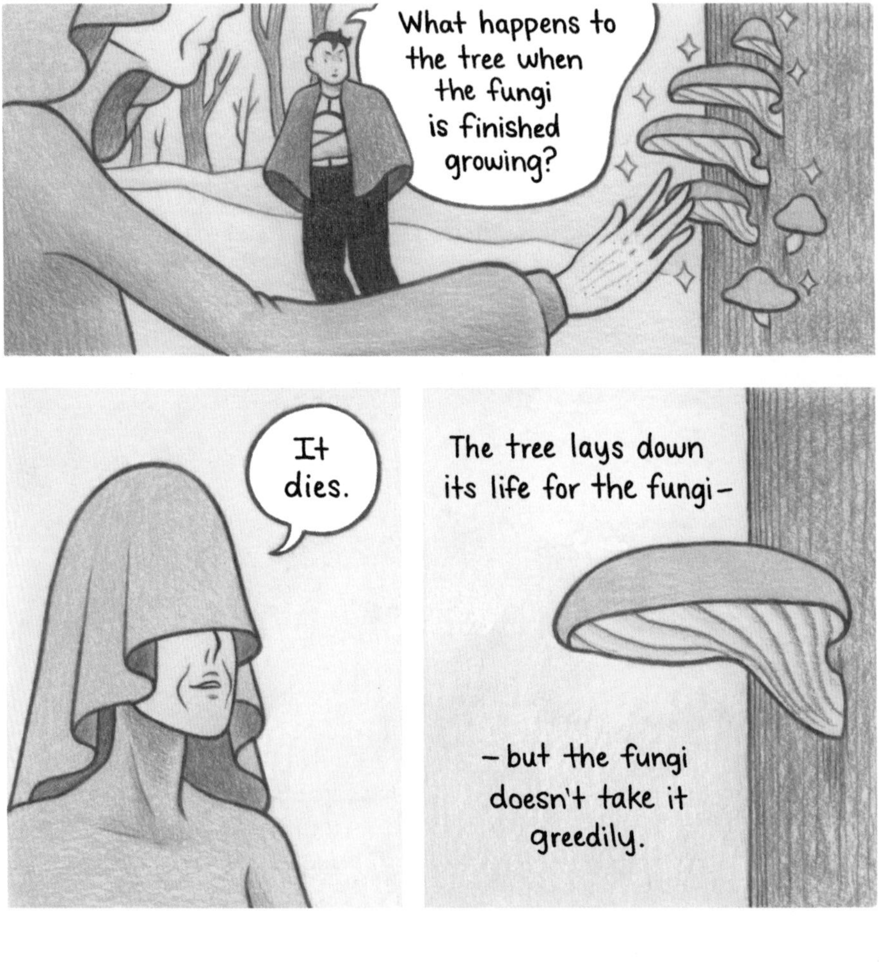
What happens to the tree when the fungi is finished growing?
It dies.
The tree lays down its life for the fungi-
-but the fungi doesn't take it greedily.

The fungi breaks down the tree and returns it to the soil.

Enriching the very place where the tree's children will grow.

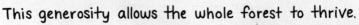

This generosity allows the whole forest to thrive.

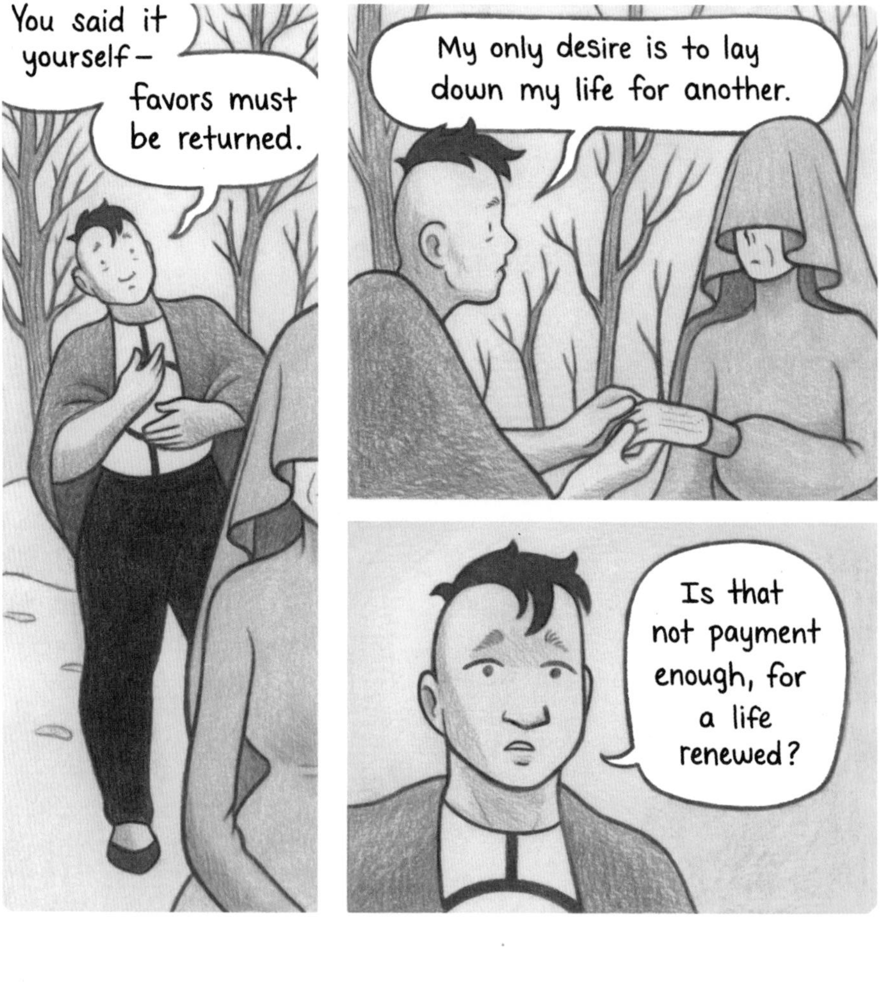
You said it yourself—
favors must be returned.
My only desire is to lay down my life for another.
Is that not payment enough, for a life renewed?

Ah, look.
Onion shoots have returned.
We can gather them for soup.

Her soups became greener by the day.

But the hands that made them

soon struggled to lift the pot.

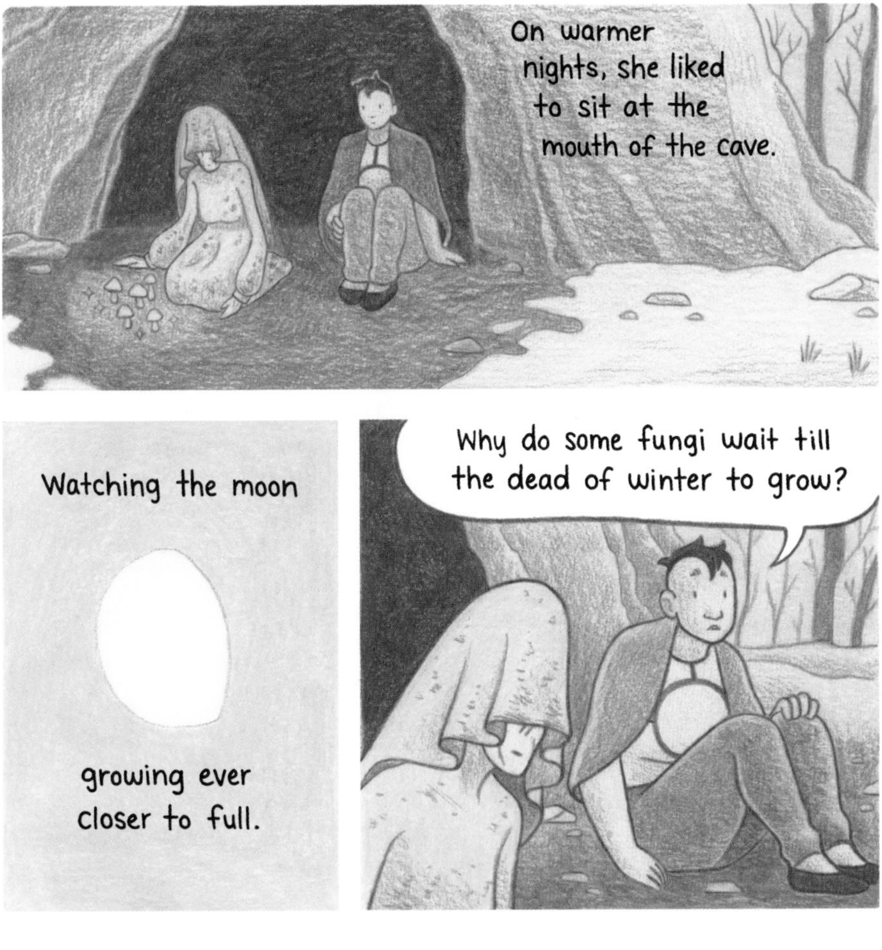
On warmer nights, she liked to sit at the mouth of the cave.
Watching the moon
growing ever closer to full.
Why do some fungi wait till the dead of winter to grow?

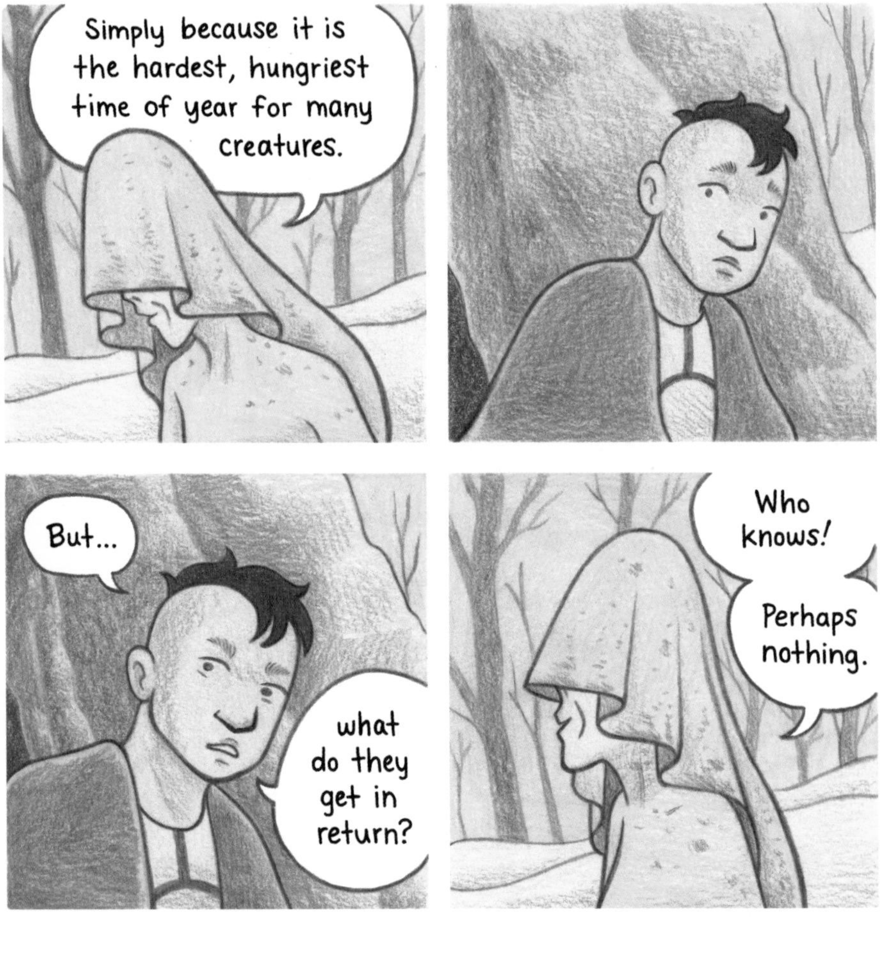
Simply because it is the hardest, hungriest time of year for many creatures.
But...
what do they get in return?
Who knows!
Perhaps nothing.

There is, however, one thing you could do for me, though.

Yes! Anything!

A dear friend of mine is waiting for me at the back of the cave.

Would you carry me to them?

I never saw anyone come in.

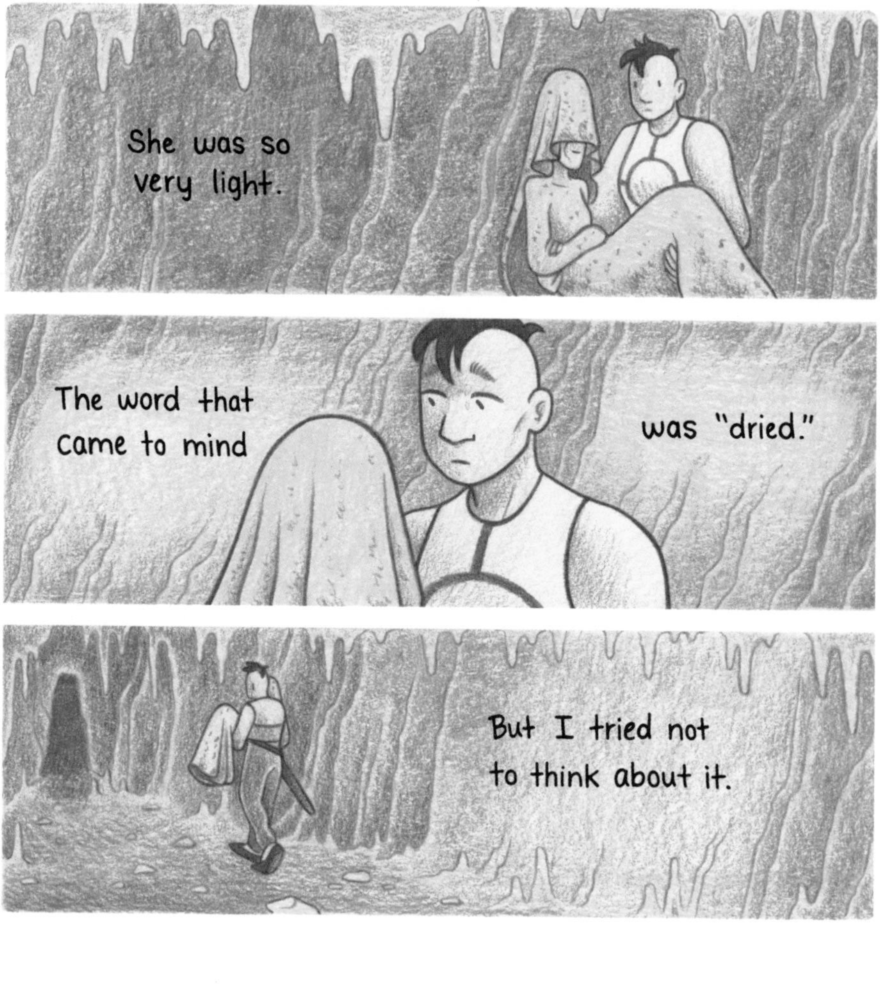
She was so very light.
The word that came to mind
was "dried."
But I tried not to think about it.

The moonlight faded as we walked.

But the path never darkened.

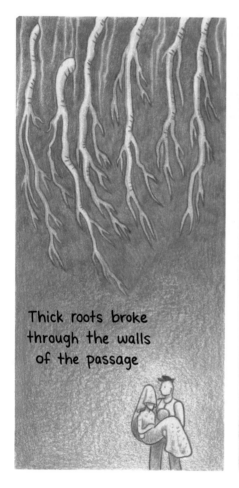

Thick roots broke
through the walls
of the passage

and waved in
some unseen
breeze.

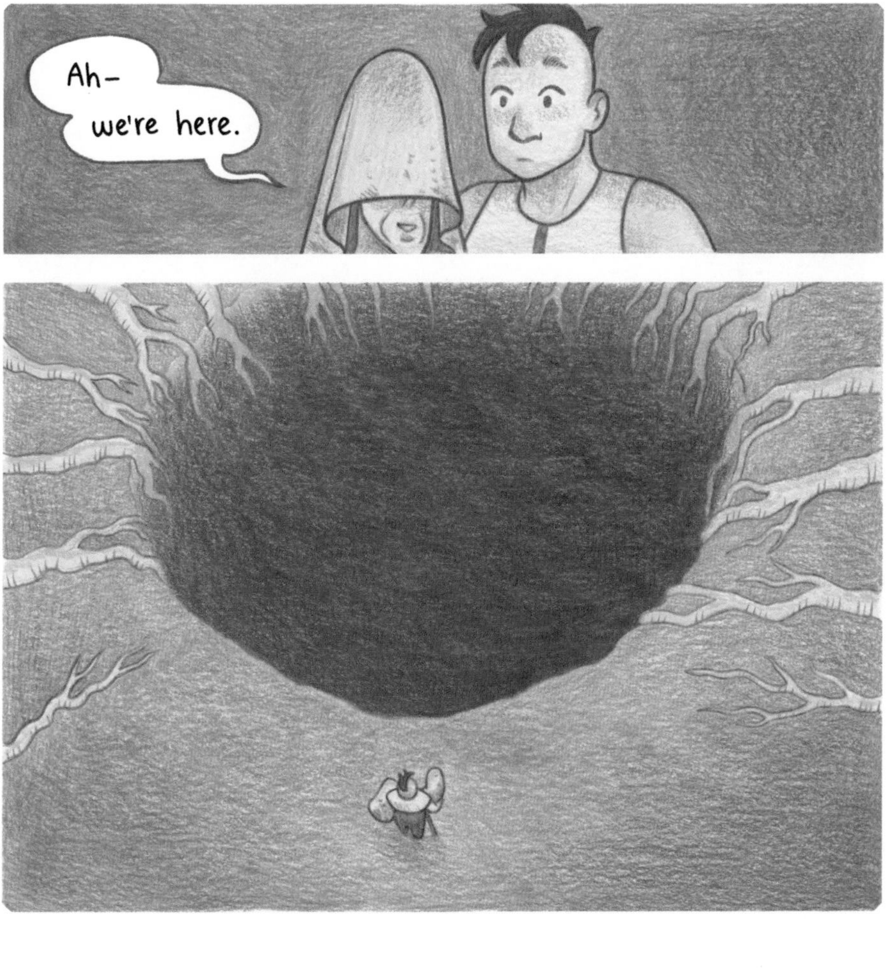
Ah-
we're here.

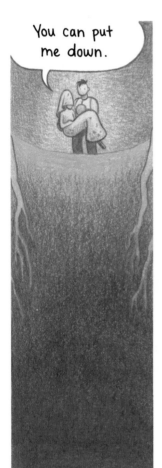

You can put me down.

Here...?

Yes.

Thank you for carrying me so far.

Wait.

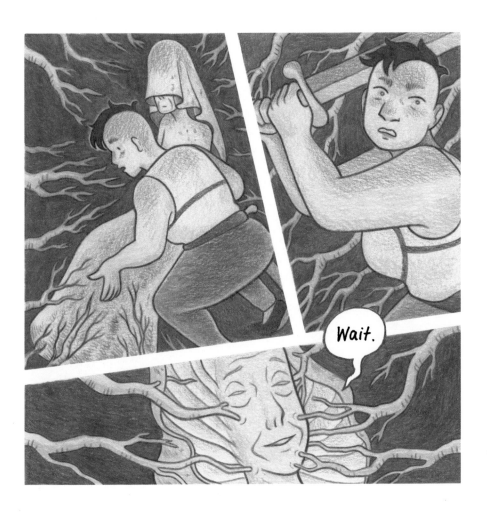

My friends are here for me.
How I've missed them!

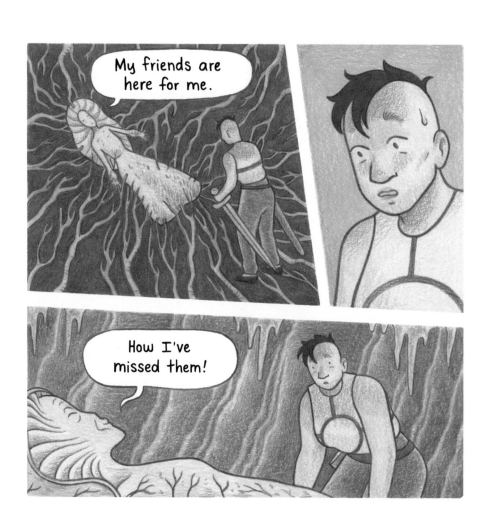

I can't just... walk away.

You can.

How am I supposed to repay you for my life?

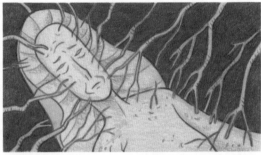

Why insist on a transaction when you're offered a gift?

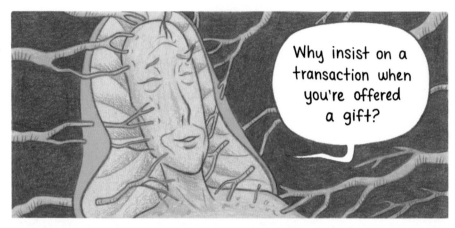

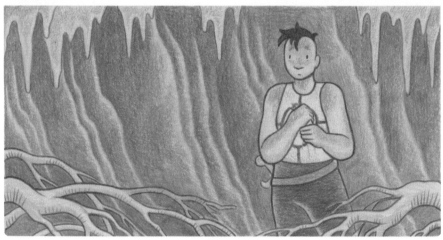

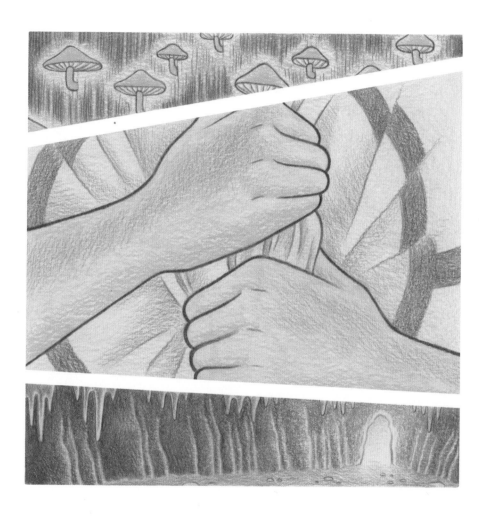

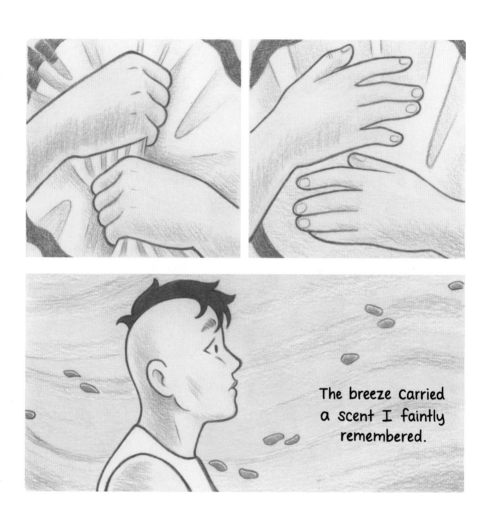

The breeze carried a scent I faintly remembered.

Somewhere,
not too far down
the path before me...

...apple trees are
blooming.

CONCLUSION

We all know
(for we are told it
so often) that girls
who linger in the woods
meet terrible fates.

They are devoured by beasts.
They lose the path.
They succumb to temptation.

They do not marry;
they do not rule.

What truly goes
hungry when it is
denied girls to devour—

—is the castle.

May we live to see
it starve.

ACKNOWLEDGMENTS

Many of the stories in this book were originally drawn as part of 24-Hour Comics Day, an annual event held on the first Saturday in October where cartoonists are challenged to complete a twenty-four-page comic in twenty-four hours. Though I broke *many* of the official rules of 24-Hour Comics Day while drawing these comics, my thanks go out to the original creators of the holiday—Scott McCloud and my former grad school professor Stephen Bissette—without whom this book may not have been possible.

I'm eternally grateful to the many people who helped make this book a reality—in particular, my agent, Jen Linnan; my editor, Gina Gagliano; and the book's designer, Patrick Crotty. Dylan Edwards provided lettering assistance on the final story in the book, which was a great help. Thanks also to all my secret Twitter comics friends who very patiently let me spam them about this book the whole time I was drawing it.

Finally, a huge thank-you to the thousands of readers who cheered me on while I drew the original twenty-four-hour stories. Your love and enthusiasm for these weird little queer fable comics kept me going during those long hours at the drawing table—and in the end became the real reason why this book is able to exist.

WITH THANKS TO IVAN BILIBIN, 1900

ABOUT THE AUTHOR

Melanie Gillman is a cartoonist and colored-pencil artist who specializes in LGBTQ books for kids and teens. They are the creator of the Stonewall Honor Award–winning graphic novel *As the Crow Flies* and *Stage Dreams*. In addition to their graphic novel work, they teach in the comics master of fine arts program at California College of the Arts.

@melgillman

GRAPHIC NOVELS FOR EVERY YA READER